UNTOLD DECADES

Stonewall Inn Editions

Michael Denneny, General Editor

UNTOLD DECADES

SEVEN COMEDIES
OF GAY ROMANCE

ROBERT
PATRICK

ST. MARTIN'S PRESS
NEW YORK

All photos by Robert Patrick.

UNTOLD DECADES. Copyright © 1988 by Robert Patrick O'Connor. All rights reserved. Printed in the United States of America.
No part of this book may be used or reproduced in any manner
whatsoever without written permission except in the case of brief
quotations embodied in critical articles or reviews. For informa-
tion, address St. Martin's Press, 175 Fifth Avenue, New York,
N.Y. 10010.

Design by Richard Oriolo

Library of Congress Cataloging-in-Publication Data

Patrick, Robert.
     Untold decades : seven comedies of gay romance /
Robert Patrick ;
    introduction by Harvey Fierstein ; foreword by William M.
Hoffman.
        p. cm.—(Stonewall Inn editions)
     ISBN 0-312-03447-4
      1. Gay men—Drama. I. Title.   II. Series.
   PS3566.A786U5 1989
   812'.54—dc20   89-10351
                                       CIP

First Edition

10 9 8 7 6 5 4 3 2 1

UNTOLD DECADES
FOR ALL THE KIDS TO COME

If I were loved, as I desire to be,
What is there in the great sphere of the earth,
And range of evil between death and birth,
That I should fear,—If I were loved by thee?

LORD ALFRED TENNYSON, *Sonnet X*

CONTENTS

FOREWORD

by William M. Hoffman

I'm not sure exactly how or when I first met Robert Patrick. It was in the Caffe Cino days, 1963 or '64. By day I was an editor at Hill and Wang, the drama book publishers, and at night I was hanging out in the cafe-theater world that preceded what came to be called "Off-Off-Broadway." I didn't know it, of course, but I was about to run off with the circus: I would quit publishing and move to the Village and become a coffeeshop playwright.

Bob wasn't called Robert Patrick then; Lanford Wilson, who had just started writing plays for the Cino, and his friend, the actor/director Michael Warren Powell, introduced him to me as Una O'Connor. I think Una was working as a typist for the city morgue at the time. He was thin (we were all thin then), and he smoked Kools (we all smoked then), and was vastly erudite about contemporary painting and the newly emerging field of pop culture.

I remember that we hung out in Greek greasy spoons—Bob, Lance, Michael, Marshall W. Mason, and myself. Bob would hypnotize us with a frame-by-frame recreation of a Betty Grable musical and link it somehow to the philosophy of Ayn Rand. (He was reading *Atlas Shrugged* for the third time.) Or he would tell us about Salvador Dali's newest painting, wondering if there were a theatrical equivalent for it. Or he would tell us what it was like to be the only gay in Roswell, New Mexico.

Actually, I'm not a very good source for sixties theater lore—

I was on speed and boilermakers—but I have a memory of Bob being completely covered with wheat paste. The Cino group was plastering the West Village with 11-by-16-inch posters. It could have been for *The Madness of Lady Bright*, Lance's revolutionary play about an aging queen, which opened in May 1964, or Bob's *Haunted Host* (November 1964), or my own first play about a gay man, *Good Night, I Love You* (September 1965). It seems so long ago. That's probably because it *is* so long ago.

I remember *The Haunted Host* in detail because I was in it. Marshall directed it fearlessly and Bob dazzled as Jay, the host of the title. It is fitting that the author himself played the first in a long line of Patrick heroes, a brilliant, misunderstood gay writer looking for love and understanding in a world that treasures neither.

I played a shallow, good-looking young man who comes to Jay's house to have his ashes hauled but has his values hauled instead. I couldn't remember my lines, no matter how much Bob and Marshall coached me. Realizing that I hadn't a shred of talent as an actor and jealous of the attention that Bob and Lanford were receiving, I wrote my first play shortly afterward.

I don't think we invented gay plays at the Caffe Cino. Perhaps Christopher Marlowe did in *Edward II* or Mae West in *The Drag*, but I think we reinvented it for ourselves. Speaking only for me, I wasn't looking to do anything political; I just wanted to write about *all* the kinds of people I knew and loved, and that turned out to be very political.

In 1963 it was hard to write about gays. It made you nervous. I have memories of gay bars with red lights that were lit whenever anyone suspected of being a cop entered. Suddenly the queens and dykes would grab each other and start dancing just as "Miss Lily Law" came in. I remember that Bob, Marshall, and I were jumped right around the corner from the Cino on Bleecker Street by fifteen teenagers screaming, "Kill the queers!" I'm glad to say the little bastards barely got away with their lives.

This was the atmosphere surrounding our first efforts portraying gays' lives. I wish I could say that things have changed enormously for gays since then, but the violence and terror are still there. What has changed is that some people are more aware of the problems and understand that the only way that the world is going to change is through gays talking about their lives and taking action (both private and collective) to improve them.

Robert Patrick was among the first to depict gay people and remains one of the best. *Untold Decades* tells the truth about our lives. I know—I was there.

WILLIAM M. HOFFMAN
April 12, 1988, New York City

PREFACE

I grew up in the Southwest watching blushing classics professors thumb through Catullus, looking for passages they dared assign us. Nights, I was collating my Tab Hunter photo collection and rolling with lovers on my dormitory cot.

Outside of town, the truckers knew where to park and wait for the local businessmen. On the poignant prairies, the cowboys kept one corner of the bunkhouse blanketed off for private whoop-de-doo.

As little boys, I and my chums had slipped into dovecotes, air-conditioning cases, and the bee-buzzing bushes around the cemetery for our Ganymedean games.

Later, like teenage laddies everywhere, we coined the euphemism, "slumber party." Those in the mood would wait until the others achieved, or feigned, sleep, then shuck off our fifties white jockey-shorts and make the bedsprings bounce.

Omnipresent were accommodating servicemen, scoutmasters, ministers, schoolteachers, and lonely laborers available for assignations in various vestries, culverts, back rows, stockrooms, and pickup trucks.

Never a word was said by day, never a wink broadcast. Students "roomed together," athletes "went camping," workingmen "had buddies," religious types "went on retreat," and the whole town knew what was happening between the projectionist and the popcorn boy and the whole town pretended it wasn't.

It wasn't just gay sex. In spite of mounting tolls of schoolgirl pregnancy and epidemic V.D., it was understood that no American had sex outside of marriage. Only those "caught" were acknowledged.

But gays were seldom even caught. Two or three students a year disappeared from college with bandaged wrists and the explanation that they "had problems." Their "best friends" suddenly dated any available woman, got one conspicuously pregnant, and staged a much-discussed wedding as the background of the story faded away.

We were not alone. Atheists, socialists, intellectuals, artists, and any member of a nonwhite race who was neither an entertainer nor a Nobel Prize winner were essentially culturally invisible.

It was a "podpeople" world, most of life a twilight zone. God, it was stupid! It couldn't get worse, and a lot of us were determined it had to get better.

A reader, and paranoid, like most abused children, I pieced together from vagrant footnotes and veiled allusions the knowledge that there had always been men like me; that we were just like other men, except that we tended to be a bit more creative and a lot less competitive, and that the whole Judeo-Christian junkpile I was hatched in was stark-raving schizophrenic and very dangerous.

I tried the Army, I tried an asylum, I tried Santa Fe's boozing Bohemia. The Army rejected me, the psychiatrists told me to move to a big town, and the Santa Fe colony was scandalized when I tried to fight for Amerindian rights.

Like many another yearning youth with nowhere to go, I Greyhounded it to New York, where if there was not truth and justice, I figured there would at least be lots of available men.

I met here the kind of brave and brazen gay men I longed for, but half the time they were so crippled by identity crises and simple self-hatred that they couldn't maintain an affectionate erection, much less a relationship.

There was society, but not safety, in numbers. Those of us who insisted on living openly gay—nobody was putting the lid back on us once we escaped from our Bible Belt garbage cans— were subject to sneers, street attacks, and once, memorably, a New

York taxi driver, who plowed down two parking meters and a lamppost on West Fourth Street trying to run over me and two boldly blond men.

Bars and baths prospered as the flood of emigrants swelled. Anonymous sex was the rule because people who couldn't face themselves couldn't face each other. One had friends and one had lovers, seldom hyphenated. Sado-masochism filtered in from the straight world and became chic. Creative people foundered in camp and psychoanalysis.

I got mad. There was nothing wrong with me and my lovers except that we had been made to think something was wrong with us!

I grew sick to death of the sickness and death of our society. I loved being sucked, but I hated being sucked into whirlpools of rationale and rotten religion just because I wanted to pair-bond pleasurably with some meaningful man who was so busy propitiating the lares and penates of Muddle America that anything handy, including my sensitive sections, was just meat for the altar of his grubby little gods.

I was sick of being punished on behalf of Jesus and Jehovah (and Allah and Stalin and Freud's fuddled followers). I was sick of erotically alienated autophobes who kept jamming Joan Crawford and Judy Garland (later David Bowie and Divine) between me and them.

The Boys in the Band was no fantasy. It still isn't, for that matter. The style has changed from Joan Crawford to *GQ*, and the god being propitiated has changed from Moses to Madison Avenue. However, conformity to the enormity persists, and whereas the straight censors once scathed one for admitting that there were gay people, the gay political press now chastizes one for writing about gay life as it is, instead of as they wish it were. Most gay men still have not realized that you cannot give yourself to someone else until you belong to yourself, and that our holes and poles are our own. Well, you can't, and they are, and I have at least had the podium of gay theater to say so for twenty-four years to those who are not so deafened by the sound of their demons that they cannot hear, take heart, and hail.

For I was very lucky. I stumbled off my Greyhound into a Greenwich Village oasis called the Caffe Cino, the first Off-Off-

Broadway theater and an Edith Cavell-type, no-questions-asked infirmary for the valiant victims of Amerika's social and sexual savagery. Joe Cino, who gave his Caffe's floor for our plays and the balm of his love for our wounds, was himself a troubled Italian Catholic who was for a time able to separate from his sickness sufficiently to grant us a space to start trying to heal it.

Because of him, a crew of dramatic Displaced Persons found a camp to concentrate in. We latter-day Roger Smiths (the patron saint of this country) found through Joe Cino a providence from which to make our contributions to the radical revolution of the sixties. So, today, along with gay pride, gay plagues and gay bowling leagues, gay politics and a gay press, there is gay theater.

This collection consists of seven short plays about gay male life in seven decades of this century, in towns small and large, among men educated and ignorant, in relationships erotic, economic, tragic, and comic.

I was as sexually active as I could manage during five of those decades, and I have always been an attentive listener to any story that involved one man getting into another man's pants. All these stories are true; some are even factual.

Do they tell the whole story? Of course not! When a tenth (or sixth, or whatever statistic you accept) of a population is forced to evolve in secret little cells with communication dangerous and indictable, multifarious customs and commitments develop. We are just beginning to learn, through memoirs, novels, diaries, surveys, gossip, and scholarship, some tiniest part of what went on betwixt man and man in this immense, illiterate, hypocritical miracle called America. Most of what has passed we will never know.

Here are glimpses I had, or images I gleaned. They reflect not only my limits of knowledge, but my limits of interest. I don't like villains, and I don't like dull people. I think conflicting ideas of good are more interesting than conflicts between good and evil. I enjoy witty, romantic people, and I love good talk.

In addition, I had a theme and structure in mind that automatically winnowed the material for this suite. My theme here is the effects of repression upon the noble spirit, and I picked the stories to trace it. I know ten thousand more gay stories, have told a lot of them, and will tell, I hope, many more. I'll get to the slumber parties and gay synagogues, believe me.

A word: those who saw *50s 60s 70s 80s* produced in New York or Hollywood will notice that the original 80s play, *Sit-Com*, has been replaced here by another. *Sit-Com* was composed in 1980, when it seemed the decade was going to center on liberated gay men's discovery of the simple, everyday facts of living and loving together that have always been such common stock for heterosexual comedy. AIDS having spread its pulpy wings over the age, *Sit-Com* seemed inappropriate, however hilarious. So it is replaced here by a new piece, *Pouf Positive*, whose origin will become clear to the reader from internal evidence.

I should like to thank Terry Helbing of Gay Theatre Alliance for a commission that resulted in three of these plays, Jeff Corrick for the use of his Kaypro II word processor to write some others, Mark Waren for the title of the book, and all the artists, artisans, and producers who have participated in their theatrical presentations; their names and roles are listed in the appendix. And I must thank Carol Nelson, or she'll hurt me.

INTRODUCTION

by Harvey Fierstein

I glowed and trembled with triumph as I stood center stage of the deserted theater. It was January 1975, opening night of Robert Patrick's *The Haunted Host*, at the Theatre on the Square in Cambridge, Massachusetts. This was my first real starring role, my first real professional appearance, my first acting job out of drag.

The reviews, just in, were wonderful. Everyone else was partying fervently in a room on another floor of the building. I had been asked to return to the stage in order that a "Victory" photo might be taken of the playwright and myself. I was the first to arrive, followed by a small mob of camera-toting reporters, gleefully drunken producers, and self-satisfied press agents. I basked in the attention and stage lights patiently awaiting my author.

He arrived. I saw Robert Patrick running down the aisle, hands outstretched toward me, and naturally I opened my arms to accept his grateful embrace. Leaping to the stage, he threw his hands around my neck, wrestled me to the floor and, sitting atop my chest, throttled me for the flashing cameras.

Lying there, smiling blithely in focus, I had time to reflect on the nature of the Playwright/Actor relationship. An Actor displeased with the work of his or her playwright has many courses of action from which to choose. Among the most popular choices are mumbling the offending line, screaming it unintelligibly, or simply forgetting to speak it. The Playwright displeased with an Actor has but two options: cut the line or kill the Actor. Mr. Patrick, justly, made his choice. It was at this moment that I decided to take my own playwrighting more seriously. Not just because I envied his position in this relationship, but because I felt myself ready to take on the "live or die" responsibilities of characters as well as actors.

Photographers gone, I thanked Robert for this lesson well taught, this example bravely set.

Joking aside, my association with Robert over the years has taught me a great many lessons about writing, acting, and living. Robert is a truly *individual* individual with a life force and energy so intense that it is sometimes frightening. To consider the catalog of his works is to be in awe. The number of published and produced pieces alone is enough to make the most prolific writer feel lazy, but then there are the variety of forms and the breadth of subjects. Robert writes One Act plays and Two Act plays and Full Length plays and Musicals. He writes Theater Criticism, Letters to the Editor and Sociological Diaries. He's written Historical Farce and Science Fiction and Poetry and Travel Magazine Articles . . .

Obviously, Mr. Patrick's droll wit, stinging insights, and seemingly limitless imagination are his talents. His greatest accomplishment though, in my opinion, is the freedom with which he writes. Through the many years of writing he has trained and practiced and honed his mind away from the restraints, restrictions, and doubts that most writers battle on a line-to-line basis. Robert thinks— Robert writes. This unfettered Art produces a fluidity and abandon that sweeps the Reader up and away. Reading or Acting one of his plays is not the time to think about it. You must allow the reasoning and reacting to be done for you, or you will be left behind. Robert Patrick is a man of few pauses. He writes on an express track. Stop to admire a twist of phrase or point of truth and you will find yourself two turns behind.

There is a constant battle that rages within us all. The subconscious mind is a din of arguing, reasoning, experiencing voices. Robert has learned how to open his ear to this world. Almost possessed, he taps into this drama of the imagination and, putting pen to paper, transcribes the experience for the rest of us. This is writ-

ing: conscious and unconscious working together, imagination un-
chained, writer unafraid to expose his secret universe.

Happily, Robert has done this again for us now. You will turn
this page and enter the rapids of his mind. I advise you to sit back
and relax. There's no more for you to do than enjoy.

1920s

▭▪▭

ONE OF THOSE
PEOPLE

for Ed Ramage

ONE OF THOSE PEOPLE

The setting is the terrace of a house in the American Midwest, sometime in the 1920s. The time is evening, and a lovely evening it is: moonlight pours through elderly oak trees. Recorded music is heard from within. It is the particularly sentimental and exotic sort of music usually played by a movie-house pianist during the seething desert-romance films of the period.

No wonder a tastefully tuxedoed MAN *escapes from the house onto the terrace, where the music can only be heard faintly. He comes to the railing of the terrace, takes out a unique cigarette case, lights a Melachrino, and laughs quietly at a joke that we will soon share.*

Not laughing at all is RALPH, *the handsome young man in an equally tasteful tuxedo, who comes huffing onto the terrace, clearly displaying high offense to anyone who might be watching. In case no one is watching,* RALPH *huskily says, "Really!" to the overly ornate terrace furniture. The* MAN *hears and turns.*

MAN
Oh, hello.

RALPH
Oh! Hello. I was . . . looking for our hosts. To say goodnight.

MAN
Please don't go.

RALPH

Oh ... Very well.

(With a becoming blush)

I wasn't really going to, I think.

(Offers his cigarette case)

Cigarette?

MAN (Displaying his lit one).

Thank you.

(Whips out his case with great style)

Have one of mine?

RALPH (Takes one).

Thank you.

(The MAN gives him a light)

What an unusual case.

MAN (Pocketing his case).

Yes, aren't they?

RALPH (Laughs a bit despite himself).

Yes, rather. But I meant—

MAN

I know what you meant. Forgive my nervous pseudo-wit. I'm feeling very uncomfortable, as I'm sure you are.

RALPH

Yes, rather.

MAN

I'm afraid my two friends in there have been up to some maladroit
matchmaking. I'm awfully sorry, and I apologize for them.

RALPH

Thank you. It isn't necessary. I never for a moment thought you
had anything to do with it.

MAN

That's very decent of you. I hadn't, of course. And it was obvious you hadn't been made privy to the scheme. Shall we just forget it and ... be friends?

RALPH

Let's. I'd like that. You're so like the characters in your books and plays. I'm a great admirer of your writing, and I was so pleased when I heard that you'd be here.

MAN

I couldn't refuse. Freddy and Anselmo are very dear old friends.

RALPH *(With some wonder)*.

Of yours, though?

MAN

Yes. We spent much time together in Berlin and Málaga when they first met. I always see them when fate brings me back to Eaton Falls.

RALPH

I believe you have people here, don't you?

MAN

Only family. No one closer than that.

RALPH

It's extraordinary that ... you ... came out of Ohio.

MAN

Not so extraordinary as if I had stayed.

RALPH

I know what you mean. I don't think I can stand it another day.

MAN

Do you plan to get away?

RALPH *(Passionately)*.

God, yes!

(Recovering his calm)

I've wheedled myself college in the East. Yale, I think. I shall have
to come on holidays for a few years, and after that I'm off to the
Continent.

MAN

Europe, that is?

RALPH

Yes. Even the Middle East, and Africa, and Asia. I want to go back
to the childhood of the race and erase my own. Do you think that's
frivolous?

MAN

It is beautiful, therefore it must be good. How do you propose to
finance this heroic hegira?

RALPH

That'll be no problem once I'm twenty-one. Until then, I'm in the
fiscal talons of my family. I don't know how I shall bear it.

MAN

Very well, I imagine. You seem to have great spirit.

RALPH *(With another becoming blush).*

Coming from you, that's an accolade. Thank you.

MAN

You have charming wit, and beautiful hands. I'm sure you'll be fine
wherever you go.

RALPH

You didn't have such an easy time getting out of here, did you?
Or am I prying?

MAN

You are, but unobjectionably. I was not blessed with particular
pecuniary fortune, no. But my and the town's combined will that I
should be elsewhere, if at all, encouraged me to achieve escape
velocity. In brief, I peddled my papers until my parlor recitations
and soft-shoe dancing attracted supporters who contrived to con-
vey me to an academy for the dramatic arts. I did not have to resort

to such devices as joining a touring troupe portraying Little Lord Fauntleroy, or blackmailing the mayor with the complicity of his colored concubine, or any of the various nefarious ploys generally associated in cheap fiction with the jettisoning of one's parochial baggage.

RALPH

You were so lucky to have talent.

MAN

Frankly, had I not, I was ready to hop a freight and prostitute myself to rich bankers, like the heroes of Horatio Alger.

RALPH *(With a winning laugh).*
I could listen to you talk forever.

MAN

You may feel you already have done. May I ask in return how you came to acquire your conspicuous sophistication here within sound of the furniture factory's whistle?

RALPH *(Delighted to talk about himself).*
I was drilled in good manners by Grandmama, who'd met the Prince of Wales and found him so disappointing that she was determined to uphold the gentility the Royal Family had let drop. Grandpapa taught me to ride, which gives an understanding of posture, and the shirt advertisements gave hints on how to dress. And of course, your stories and plays have become available, so now every aspiring dandy in these here States can have the Boy's Own Manual of Suavity ever at hand.

MAN

Hmmm. If the way you wove that compliment into your autobiography was characteristic, you have graduated cum laude. Thank you, and bravo. I feel I should sign you and exhibit you as my best work.

RALPH

What fun! If you'll autograph it, I shall never launder this cuff again!

MAN

I never carry a pen. Hostesses worldwide censor their table talk at the sight of a writing instrument.

RALPH

You really are a person who has been everywhere, aren't you?

MAN

While not fond of the term *has been* in any context, nevertheless, yes, everywhere is where I have principally been.

RALPH

It must be marvelous, banging about the globe, independent, living on your own work, and able to work anywhere you go.

MAN

It is so far, yes. I've just banged about the Orient making a comedy for London next season and a packet of songs which I may introduce in Paris, or string together for a shipboard revue.

RALPH

And you've a romance opening in New York this fall, haven't you?

MAN

I desperately hope so. *Vanity Fair* assures me that I do. If I should not, I don't think Ethel or Tallulah will speak to me again.

RALPH *(Very impressed)*.

Are they to be in it?

MAN

Only in the audience. I'm slated to sit between them at the first night and serve as a buffer.

RALPH

You really do know all of those people, of course. It's extraordinary. I mean, you're one of those people yourself, but . . . golly . . . well, they're not from Eaton Falls, so it all seems even more magical. Than it would seem otherwise. Gosh, I've gone all tongue-twisted. I am so sorry.

MAN

One needn't walk verbal tightropes all the time. It cheapens the feat.

RALPH

But around you, one feels challenged to perform.

MAN

I suppose I do see the very best of most people.

RALPH

I'm afraid *I* was not at my best inside just now. I was awfully embarrassed by the way your friends were treating us. When I saw that there was no one else expected, and they laid that amazing Arabian music on—

MAN *(Gently, but firmly)*.

Freddy, also a product of Eaton Falls, stayed home, and attended far too many flickers. When at last a legacy let him go a-wandering, he encountered Anselmo at a cinema in Berlin, in the popularly priced seats. A taste for cinematic romance drew them together. They've houses like this in Málaga and Cannes, complete with the tapestries and gramophones. They are dears, and harmless if not taken into the better homes. I can relax here and be myself. Such things, you will learn, are not unimportant, and sincerity and sweetness such as theirs are hard to find.

RALPH *(Somewhat chastened)*.

I didn't mean to insult them. It's obvious they think the world of one another, and of you.

MAN

And of you, believe me, dear boy, if they found you fit to serve up as a party favor to *me*.

RALPH

Yes. Yes, I'm sure. Now you'll put me down as a boor for criticizing my hosts in their own home.

MAN

Oh, no, my dear. . . . May I call you . . . ?

RALPH

Ralph. Please do.

MAN

Unless you intend to change it?

RALPH

I have thought so, but have decided on nothing yet.

MAN

Ralph then. My dear Ralph: For people like us it is necessary to be a bit stronger, a bit smarter, more self-critical, more observant than the usual run. Whether we happen to come already enhanced with these qualities, as some have claimed, or whether our situation invests them in us, we have traditionally—and we do have a long and proud tradition—been a little finer, a little firmer, more sensitive and flexible than others. You're being these things instinctively now, and beautifully. But you can't know, any more than a kitten pouncing on spools can know it's preparing itself for existence in a jungle, why you'll need these disciplines. There will be times when only your own spine can support you, moments when only your own wit can inspire you, days when only exacting self-control can raise you from bed, nights when nothing but your word can impel you into society. But of all these disciplines, there is none you must hold to more sternly than to be kind and sympathetic. The easiest armor to put on is always cruelty. That armor will, indeed, see you through everything. Vicious condescension toward those without your strength can make you feel momentarily superior. But that easy armor must be foregone. Don't ever curdle that creamy brow with lines of easy disdain, or curl those lips into a popular sneer. Of all the models available, the one of gentleman in our late war is most succinct: Face what you have to face with humor, dignity, and style; protect yourself with knightly grace; have contempt for your own weakness and never encourage it in others; but never, Ralph, never for an instant permit yourself to feel anything other than pity and deepest sympathy for unfortunate comrades who have, after all, fallen in the same battle.

(Music begins to play within—a subtle, mocking rhumba)

RALPH *(Quietly).*
You make me feel ashamed.

MAN *(Kindly).*
I don't mean to.

RALPH
But, of course, you make me feel immeasurably proud, as well.
(They face one another for a moment like soldiers. Then—)
I say . . . this is a song of yours, isn't it?

MAN
Yes, from my last show. Shall I sing it for you?

RALPH
Oh, would you?

MAN
Very well.
(Sings)
"Cigarette?"
Three syllables that smother
Our shyness with each other
When we're not lovers yet.

"Have we met?"
Would be too bold and breezy.
It's more elite and easy
To say, "cigarette?"

As you all
Descend into the garden,
Lingering
Separately you stand.
A casual,
"May I beg your pardon?"
Fingering
Something in your hand.

This amulet

Provides a subtle masking
For what you're really asking
When you say, "cigarette?"

RALPH *(As the music continues)*.
Oh, that's enchanting!

MAN
There are . . . private lyrics as well.

RALPH
Oh, please sing them.

MAN *(Sings)*.
"Cigarette?"
Where palms were softly swaying,
I heard a shadow saying
To a slender silhouette.
"Not just yet,"
The silhouette half-scolded.
The cigarette case folded
Like a castanet.

It might have led
To a love affair in Paris,
The kind that ends
In little tears or little joy.
One might have said
Something to embarrass,
But now they can be friends,
Clever man and clever boy.

For etiquette
And all that was respected,
And all that was rejected
Was a cigarette.
"Cigarette?"
"Not just yet."
Cigarette—
  (Holds out his case, speaks)
Cigarette?

RALPH

You're right, of course. It was beastly of me not to appreciate what your friends—our friends—were trying to do. It was, I see now, the kindest and most thoughtful thing they could conceive of. I shall thank them profusely by letter. Would that be the right thing?

MAN *(Putting cigarette case away).*

I'm certain you need ask no one what is the right thing.

RALPH *(Blushing with pride).*

Thank you.

(With a mischievous twinkle)

All the same, you must admit . . .

MAN *(Quickly).*

Yes, yes, of course, their intention was delightfully absurd.

(With his own kind of twinkle)

And, for that matter, continues to be so.

RALPH

How do you mean?

MAN

You must have noticed that they've left us quite alone.

RALPH

Oh, good heavens, you don't suppose that they suppose . . . ?

MAN

Oh, I'm sure they do. I believe I could with a hastily borrowed pen transcribe precisely the Valentino visions simmering on the screens of their imaginations.

RALPH

I feel horribly self-conscious all of a sudden.

MAN

I'm sure they have no idea how appalling the idea is.

RALPH

Yes, quite ridiculous.

MAN

Can't you picture how it would be if we two were to feel obligated to realize their scenario?

RALPH

Hilarious, I'm sure.

MAN

I should be required to weave the most ordinary compliments comparing you to Narcissus and Hyacinthus and any mythic morsel who got himself transformed into a flower.

RALPH

And my role, I suppose, would be to mew about your work and ask you how you get your ideas, and are your characters based on reeeeal people, with all sorts of italics and inverted quotes around every simpering banality.

MAN

Quite. Then I would brush a honey-hued lock from your forehead, and mention that I should be dining alone tomorrow night at such-and-such a great hotel.

RALPH

And I must hint that I'd heard their murals were superb examples of the Byzantine or Nazarene or some such silly period.

MAN

I should cancel all my calls and cover my typewriter.

RALPH

Except for a single page left visible, with passages of stimulating dialogue?

MAN

Your first surrender, I imagine, would fall between the *crème brulée* and the Drambuie.

RALPH

Of course, I'd abandon everything to flee to Saint-Tropez with you.

MAN

Tropical days would give way to beachswept nights.

RALPH

I'd be delightfully aghast when people recognized you.

MAN

You'd change clothes a dozen times a day while I wept over the bills.

RALPH

Women would smile at you and I'd make sly, knowing little rosebud mouths.

MAN

I'd watch you with the dawn and wonder how I dared even dream such an angel might lie beside me.

RALPH

I'd sneak peeks at you over magazines and pray you'd never notice that I don't deserve you.

MAN

Soon you'd be yawning at my work and complimenting my rivals.

RALPH

Would I?

MAN

I'm afraid so.

RALPH

Well, soon you'd be fed up with my unexciting omnipresence and slip away with weak excuses, wouldn't you?

MAN

I might do. Certainly I'd find pretexts to relax with goatish beachboys and sniggering musicians.

RALPH

Well, I've no doubt I'd be found wrestling with the lifeguard.

MAN

The lifeguard?

RALPH

Studying chemical engineering, he says, and awfully keen on boating.

MAN

Oh, dear. I should become sharply ironic about your excursions.

RALPH

I would wax quite comic concerning your entourage.

MAN

Awfully decent fellows.

RALPH

If one likes that sort of thing.

MAN

Soon I'd be telling our friends I hadn't the slightest idea whether you were coming along or not.

RALPH

And I'd tell people stopping by for me, "Oh, he's in there hammering out yammer."

MAN

I should disappear for days and come back without any wallet.

RALPH

I should be found at home with three sympathetic chums whom I'd refuse to ask to go.

MAN

There'd be asinine rows over poodles and statuettes.

RALPH

I shouldn't pack a single book you'd signed for me as I filled my chic valise.

MAN

Oh, the small dinners I'd be given, in hopes I'd spill the whole true story.

RALPH

I'd check items in all the posh papers, pretending delight that we aren't mentioned.

MAN

And after two seasons, or three, we'd have a casual encounter in a cloakroom.

RALPH

All the world would be watching, but we shouldn't notice.

MAN

We'd each arch an eyebrow and ask without real disdain, "How's yours?"

RALPH

God, really? Yes, I suppose so. And I suppose Anselmo and Freddy would be riffling address books, anxious to invite us separately to intimate evenings—

MAN *(Gazing meaningfully at* RALPH*)*.

—where some unthinkably exquisite creature is the only other guest. Yes.

RALPH

I see . . . Have you really been through it so often?

MAN

As to that, let me merely say that some have suggested an international competition: Make this Man Fall in Love Again.

*(*RALPH *laughs)*

Worldwide the challenge will resound. Champions will appear from Hollywood, from Marrakesh, from Oxford, and the Midwest. Adolescent wiles will be plied on a scale undreamed of in the crassest casting offices. Vitiated youths will be carted off the field in litters. The last contestants will enter the lists paralyzed with dread. None will renounce the task; boys have to compete for *something*. But I will sit, implacable as Medusa, staring down the swarthiest sailor, the downiest schoolboy. When the carnage is complete, the stadium will empty without a sound. No one will look back. I will have become a monument to Buster Keaton—grim, chiseled, blank-faced, rinsed with a hose.

RALPH

Marvelous. Is that in your next play?

MAN

Probably.

(Music sounds within, another helping of sweltering cinematic romance)

RALPH

I suppose we should go in now.

MAN

I'm certain we should. I hear the no-nonsense gurgling of Drambuie. And I must make my farewells. I shall be leaving tomorrow.

RALPH

Oh? I . . . hadn't heard that.

MAN

I've dealt with such family bickering as was necessary. I . . . do hope I'll see you again if ever I should come through.

RALPH

Thank you. You know, it's highly likely I'm going to school in the East, and it's no distance to New York. No doubt I'll be taking in a lot of shows.

MAN

Well, if time and circumstance find you in Manhattan for my opening, and the mood moves you, do check at the box office. There'll be a ticket for you.

RALPH

How nice. And perhaps you'll let me take you for a drink after. But of course you'll be being lionized.

MAN

Nothing would be more delightful than to elude all the hounds for a drink with you. Think of the talk we will cause.

RALPH

That would be marvelous.

MAN

Yes, it will. Oh, and Ralph?

RALPH

Yes sir?

MAN

I'll leave tickets for two. Do feel free to bring a friend.

RALPH

Of course. How generous.

MAN

Not at all. Think of the talk *that* will cause!

(Laughing, they link arms and exit together into the house)

C U R T A I N

1930s

■▭·▭■

THE
RIVER JORDAN

for my father

THE RIVER JORDAN

SCENE ONE

The setting is a workingman's bar outside a small town in Texas in the 1930s. That is, it was a workingman's bar when there were working men. Now it is a place where men come and sit, and wait, and hope, or don't hope.

The walls of the long and ill-lit room are irregular slats, cheap and unpainted, gray from endless dust storms. Between them we can see the beginnings of a hellish sunset, and the silhouettes of skeletal oil derricks, long unused.

We see a rickety, hand-nailed table, mismatched wooden chairs mended with baling wire, a single weak lightbulb suspended from a wire. On the wall is a hand-scrawled sign on a piece of dirty cardboard: "You muss have wun drink or you kant stay."

Into this dry watering hole come JOHN-BO and CASDALE, about thirty and dressed in flashy suits of extreme cut, which would be described as "for motoring" in Esquire. JOHN-BO, who carries two small jelly jars containing whiskey, has been here before. CASDALE, who carries a handkerchief to his nose, has not.

JOHN-BO *(Goes to table).*

Casdale, over here, this table. This is where he comes to meet me.

CASDALE *(Staring about, disconcerted).*

Good God, John-Bo, this has got to be a joke. This isn't a bar, it's a barn or somethin'.

JOHN-BO *(Sets glasses on table, looks about).*

No, it's their bar, really.

CASDALE *(Edging close to JOHN-BO in fear).*

But you can see sunset through the slats in the walls.

JOHN-BO

Makes it easier to watch your car.

CASDALE

It's like I've been eaten by a skeleton. It's like one of those emaciated men at those tables had swallowed me!

JOHN-BO *(Scanning the place, looking for someone).*

And you were afraid we'd run into someone who knows us.

CASDALE

Someone drivin' by could still see us through the gaps in the walls. God, look out there at those sinister rusty derricks. Must've been an oilfield or somethin' before the Crash.

JOHN-BO *(Giving up search).*

Well, he's not here yet.

(Starts to sit)

CASDALE

John-Bo! Don't *sit* on that!

(Whips out handkerchief, dusts chair)

There! All of West Texas was on that chair.

(Dusts off another chair)

And all of East Texas on this one.

(They sit)

Talk about back to nature!

JOHN-BO

If you think the decor is primitive, wait 'til you taste what they drink. Here.

(He shoves a glass toward CASDALE*)*

CASDALE *(Shoves glass away).*

Fun's fun, John-Bo, but I am not drinkin' that diesel fuel.

(He surveys the bar)

My God, are these your idea of beauties? They look like unwashed El Grecos.

JOHN-BO

Oh, but this one's different, Casdale. Wait'til you see. Old English stock, I'll bet. Solid muscle, and clean, and somehow he gets the money to shave every day. You'll love him.

CASDALE *(Still surveying the inhabitants).*

Jesus, a Depression is a terrible thing. I bet some of these creatures were beautiful farmboys once. Dear God, I might have seen them when they were youths, all golden and glowin' in the sun!

JOHN-BO

You ought to see their children, dear. They're all goin' to grow up to be rickety skeletons.

CASDALE *(Reads sign on wall).*

"You muss have wun drink or you kant stay." I suppose they sit over one jar of this antifreeze all evenin'. Where do they get the money?

JOHN-BO

Not from me.

(Nostalgically)

I used to come in here when I was a boy and pick up oil workers and the odd farmhand.

CASDALE

And never told me? You hog.

JOHN-BO

But now! God. That's why this boy is such a find. Must be from very good constitution stock. You won't regret takin' him off my hands.

CASDALE

I better not. I was goin' to Juárez this weekend. You can get anything there for two dollars.

JOHN-BO

Includin' diarrhea and the old clap-clap.

CASDALE

Too true. But not if you watch what you eat.

JOHN-BO

Don't say things like that. I don't camp around this boy.

CASDALE

Well, where is he? We can't wait too long, you know.

JOHN-BO

He's sometimes late. He has a wife to lie to.

CASDALE

Oh, so he's not . . . one of us?

JOHN-BO

I never ask. You be nice. I've taken a kind of interest in the boy.

CASDALE

Yes, and I know what kind.

JOHN-BO *(Suddenly electrified)*.

Hush up. Here he comes.

*(*RAY *enters, handsome, thin, slow, relaxed, in worn, neatly patched clothes. He pauses at his entrance, taking in the fact that there are two men at the table, shrugs, and comes to table)*

CASDALE *(Whispers)*.
My God, he is lovely.

JOHN-BO *(Whispers, slaps* CASDALE's *arm)*.
Hush, here he comes.
(Rises, pulls out a chair)
Ray, over here.

RAY *(Reaches table)*.
Yeah, I know. Hello, ol' John-Bo.

JOHN-BO
My, I'm glad you could make it. I was afraid you wouldn't come.

RAY
I come. I ain't got nowheres else to go. Did you get me my drink?

CASDALE *(Awed, hands* RAY *drink)*.
Here you are, just waiting for you.

RAY *(Drains glass)*.
Which o' you is gonna get me more?

JOHN-BO *(Takes empty glass)*.
I will. You just sit right down here and relax.
*(*JOHN-BO *exits, making "get friendly" signs to* CASDALE*)*

RAY *(Sits)*.
I'm relaxed.

CASDALE *(Stands)*.
John-Bo forgot to introduce us. I'm—

JOHN-BO *(Re-entering, flustered)*.
Ray, what will you think of me? This is my friend, Cas—

CASDALE *(Whacks* JOHN-BO*)*.
Smythe. My name is Smythe.

JOHN-BO

Of course. "Smythe." He's a very good friend whom I thought you might like to meet. He's the nicest sort of person an' I know you'll enjoy each other.

RAY

Hello.

CASDALE *(Meaning it with all his heart).*

Charmed.

JOHN-BO

I'll just go an' get you that drink now.

*(*JOHN-BO *exits)*

CASDALE

John-Bo is such a type.

RAY *(Points at other whiskey on table).*

Is anyone drinkin' that?

CASDALE

My God, no! . . . I mean, no. Help yourself.

*(*RAY *drains second glass)*

My, you really do put it away, don't you? Well, I like to see a man who holds his liquor. The men of my family were famous for their ability to drink hard and shoot straight. I really admire that sort of manly man. Except in my family, of course.

RAY

Is that your car outside, the yellow one?

CASDALE

Why, yes. Do you like it? They didn't want to paint one that color. It's a Rolls. Royce. From England? Are you fond of cars? I'd love to show you how fast it can go.

RAY

I just wondered if that was where we was goin' to go.

CASDALE

Go?

RAY

It don't look like the back seat is very big in it.

CASDALE

Well, actually it's not. But it has a very smooth ride. Even over these washboard roads. Continental engineerin', you know. I'd be delighted to take you for a spin. John-Bo, unfortunately, has had somethin' come up that is goin' to keep him from your engagement, so he asked if I could come with him to pick you up, an' then I thought perhaps we could drop him off at—or near—his appointment an' I might show you how beautifully the car functions. If you like.

RAY *(With only a small sigh)*.

Then have you got someplace for us to go to?

CASDALE

I beg your pardon?

RAY

Have you got any place for us to go to?

CASDALE *(Sits)*.

Well, funny you should mention it. I do have a little country place not all that far from here where Daddy used to shoot. It's quite quaint architecturally, an' awfully comfortable, very rugged, but quite interestin', really, an' I—

(During this speech, JOHN-BO *has entered with two more drinks and sits at table)*

RAY *(Takes a drink and starts sipping)*.

John-Bo, didn't you tell him about me?

JOHN-BO

Well, actually, I didn't have time to—

CASDALE

John-Bo said you were a very nice fellow, and that he thought you and I—

RAY *(Stands, but merely to gain attention, with no show of anger or impatience).*

Listen, you don't have to do any this stuff with me. Ever'thing's okay. You don't have to show me your fancy car or tell me how bigtime your family is, or nothin' like that. It's okay. Just . . . buy me enough whiskey to get me drunk, an' get me out o' here without too much commotion, an' you can whang me or bang me or whatever you got in mind. An' slip some money in my pocket: shirt pocket with the button on it, an' make sure it's tight buttoned. An' then make sure I'm standin' up an' let me out at the corner of Flagstaff an' Nineteenth, an' point me east, okay? Just make sure I get drunk. That's all I ask you to do.

(Gulps half of drink)

CASDALE *(After he and* JOHN-BO *sit speechless for a moment).*

Well, my, you're certainly frank, aren't you? That's very refreshing.

JOHN-BO

You see, Ray, I have to go somewhere tonight. I wish I could tell you where, but you see—

RAY

It's okay. It don't make no difference. Don't nobody care who nobody is here. We're here for what we're here for. At least we don't have to mess one another up pretendin'.

(Sits and finishes drink)

JOHN-BO

Oh, Ray, let me try to explain—

CASDALE *(Shushes* JOHN-BO *with one hand, hands* RAY *drink with the other).*

It's all right, John-Bo. You can go. He's right. I'll get along just fine with Ray. I think we understand each other.

*(*AEGIS *enters and looks about, quickly spotting the table. He is in his*

thirties, suave, handsome, dressed with subtle taste and style, and altogether a different breed from CASDALE *and* JOHN-BO. AEGIS *bears himself with great dignity and discipline. He advances matter-of-factly to the table.)*

AEGIS

John-Bo. I saw Casdale's car. I was on my way to pick you up. Is this your bachelor party?

CASDALE

Aegis. My God, who else is here?

AEGIS

Easy, Cas, it's only me.
(With easy humor)

John-Bo, is that what you're wearing to your wedding rehearsal? Your *Presbyterian* wedding rehearsal?
(RAY laughs)

JOHN-BO

Aegis. Hello. No. I have my full dress suit in the back of ... uh ...
(Cannot remember the name Smythe)

RAY *(Matter-of-factly)*.

Smythe's.

JOHN-BO

Smythe's car. Yes.

AEGIS

Well, go put it in mine, pig-brain. We'll go straight from here. You can change in the vestry with the handmaidens.

JOHN-BO

Uh—

AEGIS

Go ahead, transfer your suit. I'll have a drink.

JOHN-BO *(Stands)*.
Well, all right, but—

AEGIS *(With quiet authority)*.
Go, John-Bo. Now.

JOHN-BO *(Dusting the seat of his pants as he exits)*.
Just watch yourself sittin' down, all right?
*(*JOHN-BO *exits)*

AEGIS *(Sits carelessly, looks about, not unamused by the situation, especially the terrified* CASDALE*)*.
I don't suppose they have table service here?

RAY *(Grinning a bit, feeling his liquor)*.
Not for drinks, they don't.

CASDALE
No, you have to get your own.

AEGIS
Oh, I'll bet I could talk you into getting me one, couldn't I, uh . . . what *was* that name again?

CASDALE *(Can't remember Smythe)*.
Uh . . . uh . . .

RAY *(Simply)*.
Smythe.

AEGIS
Couldn't I . . . Smythe?

RAY *(Stands)*.
I'll go get drinks if one of you'll give me the money.

AEGIS
No, let Smythe play lackey for us while we talk. And what's your name?

RAY

Ray.

AEGIS

Hello, Ray.

CASDALE *(Stands).*

I'll see if they've got somethin' a human bein' can drink.
(Exits, reluctantly)

AEGIS *(With great tact).*

Ray . . . are these fellows . . . bothering you in any way?

RAY

What fellows?

AEGIS

John-Bo and Casdale.

RAY *(With a wee grin, sits).*

Smythe.

AEGIS

I'll get him out of here, too, if you like. It's no trouble.

RAY *(Suddenly serious).*

No.

AEGIS

Have you . . . met them before?

RAY

It's okay.

AEGIS

Pardon me for intruding. I only wanted to—

RAY

It's okay. Ever'thing's okay.

AEGIS

Well, if you say so. I could take them both with me.

RAY *(Almost shouts).*

Don't!

(More quietly)

Please.

AEGIS

You seem like rather a nice chap. I don't know if you know what you're involved in. I'm not sure that I ought to—

RAY *(Insistent).*

No, you don't need to. Ever'thing's okay just like it is.

AEGIS

I was only trying to—

RAY

Oh, Mister, let us alone, okay? They ain't nothin' wrong an' ain't nobody botherin' nobody. Things is what they is, an' you got some kind o' party to go to. I got me a party to go to, too. So thank you for what you're tryin' to do, but talkin' like this makes the whiskey let go o' me, an' I'm gonna need to be drunk, so please don't make me talk nor explain no more, okay? You go your way an' I'll go—

(CASDALE returns with three tequilas)

—his way.

CASDALE *(Sets drinks on table and sits).*

Well, I'm afraid the limit of their sophistication is tequila. It's not good, but it's exotic. Did I actually see you two talkin'?

RAY *(Trying for a party mood).*

Thanks, Smythe, thanks a lot.

(Takes glass and empties it in one huge gulp)

CASDALE *(Watching with his awe turning to anxiety).*

Have you *had* tequila?

RAY *(Feeling it quickly).*

It's fine. It's real strong. It'll help me get back to where I used to was. It makes a person crazy.

(Trying to be coquettish)

How'd you know I like tequila, Smythe? That ol' John-Bo, he just buys me whiskey. I don't think he wants me crazy. He likes me kind o' quiet an' sleepy. But choor gonna like me crazy, ain't cha, Smythe? That's the kind of a guy you are!

(Slaps CASDALE on back, drains another glass)

CASDALE *(Very worried, faking cheerfulness).*

Well, Aegis, you certainly have livened our little friend up. What's your secret?

AEGIS *(With some distaste).*

Interference with the signal. Sets up static. I'll remove myself.

(He stands as JOHN-BO enters, breathless)

John-Bo, are you ready to go?

JOHN-BO

Yes, yes, I transferred my things.

RAY *(Stands, loud but friendly).*

Hey, John-Bo, don't go. Why don't choo an' ol' Smythe both stay? You an' me an' him can go off to his daddy's huntin' lodge an' get real comfortable.

(To AEGIS)

Hear that? Com-for-ta-ble with four syllables. That's what ol' John-Bo taught me first time I met him. Not cumf-ter-bull with three, but com-for-ta-ble with four syllables. Syl-la-bles, three syllables.

(To JOHN-BO)

What do you say, ol' John-Bo?

(To CASDALE)

What do you say, Smythe? Let's all go an' get ourselves com-for-ta-ble.

JOHN-BO *(Mightily tempted).*

I have somewhere I *have* to go, Ray. Aegis, we should *leave.*

RAY *(Trying to throw arms around* JOHN-BO's *and* CASDALE's *shoulders).*

Don't worry. Ain't nobody goin' to take no notice of nothin' that goes on in this corner. That's what this corner's for. For people to be private in.

CASDALE *(Worried by* RAY's *exuberance).*

John-Bo.

RAY

It's okay. I was just tryin' to be friendly. I shouldn't do that. I should just be quiet an' not draw no attention an' let things happen, okay?

(Growing sadder)

But don't worry none about any o' them guys. Them poor ol' skinny guys. They couldn't do nothin' nohow. An' they wouldn't. An' what the hell's the reason to? Huh?

AEGIS

Casdale, maybe you should go with us.

JOHN-BO

Yes, maybe we should all go.

RAY

Please don't. Okay? Please don't go. I didn't mean to embarrass no one.

CASDALE *(Frantic).*

John-Bo?

JOHN-BO

He's usually all right. I never saw him get this worked up before.

AEGIS

I think it's me. Come, John-Bo. Thy bride awaits.

(He starts to shove JOHN-BO *toward the door)*

CASDALE

John-Bo, I'm comin', too.

(Throws three bills on table)

Here's some money, Roy, Ray. I can't miss your weddin' rehearsal, John-Bo.

(CASDALE exits frantically past AEGIS and JOHN-BO)

JOHN-BO *(Terror-stricken)*.

Oh great God, he left money on the table. Right in front of people!

AEGIS

Come on, John-Bo. Let's not embarrass the boy anymore.

JOHN-BO

Yes! Yes!

(JOHN-BO flees. AEGIS follows, with a brief glance back at RAY, who has been standing unsteadily weaving throughout this madness. RAY falls into a chair and finds the remaining tequila. We hear a car starting and driving away as RAY drinks half the glass. Then he slouches back and sings, softly.)

RAY *(Sings, sadly)*.

I'm crossin' over that River Jordan.
I'm crossin' over to my heavenly home.
I'm crossin' over that sacred river,
Nevermore to ramble, nevermore to roam.

(He finishes the drink. AEGIS re-enters and stands some distance away. RAY smiles and holds the empty glass up as if ordering a refill.)

AEGIS

I sent them both away in "Smythe's" car.

(Sits)

I stayed to take you home.

RAY *(Starts third tequila)*.

You didn't have to do that.

AEGIS

I didn't want to leave you here without transportation.

RAY

It's okay. I ain't goin' to drink no more, after this last one, if that's what you're a-feared of. I don't never spend no money on whiskey. That's my one unbreakable rule. If somebody else has got it to spend, an' wants to spend it on buyin' me whiskey, then I'll drink it. But I don't never spend no money I get my hands on on no whiskey. No sir. That all goes to ... well ...

AEGIS

To what, Ray? To whom?

RAY

To whom? Tu-whoom, tu-whoom-tu-whoom.

(Takes money out of shirt pocket)

See? Smythe left me ... hey, three dollars! Whew! ... Three dollars ... That's enough to pay the rent. Hot damn. Ol' John-Bo usually just opens up my ol' pocket whilst I'm sleepin' an' slips in fifty cents.

AEGIS *(Loud, shocked)*.

Fifty cents!

RAY

Ssshhhh. Yeah, ol' John-Bo is usually good for fifty cents. An' fifty cents'll feed my wife an' kids for three days. Now, I can pay the rent with this three dollars—or I can feed my fam'ly for—let's see ...

AEGIS

Eighteen days.

RAY

Yeah, you're real quick. Eighteen days. But if I do that, then we'll lose our shack. An' we don't have nothin' to make a tent of. So I can feed 'em an' have us all sleepin' outdoors on a blanket—we got a blanket—or I can pay the rent an' listen to the children cryin' ...

ket, buttons it, and then, for the first time,

your car?

got?

got?

to find AEGIS's *car outside)*

Or you got a roomy car?

AEGIS *(With a dawning and distasteful understanding).*
I'm in my speedster. It's a small car.

RAY *(Starting to turn on the charm).*
But I bet you got some place for us to go.

AEGIS *(With restraint and dignity).*
Ray, the fact that I know those two bozos does not make me one
of them. I did not come back in here for the purpose of—

RAY
It's okay. It's okay. I got to make some more money. I don't think
I'm goin' to be seein' ol' Smythe again. An' ... hey, ol' John-Bo's
gettin' married, ain't he? Don't suppose he'll be back ... or not 'til
after the honeymoon. So. You got a place? Somewheres we can
go?

*(*AEGIS *does not answer)*
I bet you ain't married.

AEGIS

No, I'm not.

RAY

Don't know how I knowed that. Wait, yes I do know. You look like you're more honest. I can't see you makin' any woman wait. An' wonder. My first one I met here, he was married. I hated him to tell me what lies he told his woman. But it was all right because he learned to keep me drunk. Oh, by the way, I do have to be a little drunk.

AEGIS *(Takes out his wallet).*

Ray, let me give you—

RAY *(With quiet firmness).*

No! Don't do that. Not because it ain't safe here. I don't think nobody here would rob you. Hell, if they would, they wouldn't be here, would they? But see, I ain't drunk enough to take no money directly. Oh, I don't mind ol' Smythe leavin' me money, 'cause he took up my evenin' an' run away. Besides, he probably lost me ol' John-Bo, so it's okay if he pays for that. But what you're wantin' to do . . . give me money thataway . . . I can't do that yet.

(Looking around bar)

I think most o' the men in here . . . can't quite do that yet. You see them fellas? I knowed some o' them fellas since I was born. But you notice that even when ol' Smythe went off an' left me his money, I didn't stand up an' offer to buy nobody no drinks. When I was a little boy, my daddy would take me to a bar in town, an' if somebody had just got lucky gamblin' or in a rodeo, why the first thing he'd do is come in an' stand ever'body to free drinks. I used to think that was the sign of a man, to do that, to stand his buddies free drinks if he had him a stroke o' luck. But if I was to do that now, why, most o' these men'd say no. Not because o' how I come by the money; ain't a one of 'em wouldn't get money any honest way he could. But because they know I got a wife an' three kids, too. So they wouldn't let me throw it away on 'em here. No matter how lucky I get.

(Turns back to AEGIS*)*

No, mister, I can't take that. Put it away.

AEGIS *(Puts his wallet away, then speaks)*.

Ray, I'd like to help you.

RAY *(Sweetly)*.

Ooooo, then get me drunk an' take me somewheres where it's really nice, an' be nice about me. Say nice things to me an' make me feel good. Make me real happy, an' be happy to be with me. I got a wife wonders how I get the money I bring home to her, an' smells liquor on my breath when I come in mornin's an' give 'er fifty cents . . . an' knows I'd never spend money on no liquor an' do her an' the kids out o' nothin'. An' she don't ask me no questions 'cause I told her never to ask me none. An' somehow I stayed healthy an' she ain't, an' she's all skin an' bones an' she don't like for me to touch 'er . . . an' I ain't been touchin' 'er none. Take me away somewheres where we can be nice to one another an' laugh an' have some fun. Okay, mister?

AEGIS

Ray, believe me, that isn't what I came back in here for. I hate to see a nice young man like you doing this to yourself.

RAY

Mister, this ain't nothin' new. You people that live up in them houses with all them floors, you don't know what goes on. This here was Injun country, an' cowboy country, an' railroad country, an' farmer country, an' cattle country, an' oil-worker country, all in a row, an' mister, they was a hunnerd thousan' men. Where do you think they was for all them men to go to? You think they is anything new just 'cause the banks went bust an' the trains stopped an' the country's gone to dust bowl? You don't know nothin' but hidin' an' buyin' an' lyin', you poor rich people. You ever been in one o' them clapboard hotels where the workin' men stay? You ever seen them signs that says "It's twenty cents extra if your buddy spends the night?" Ah, mister, things ain't so bad as you make out they is, not between you an' me, anyways. I like you. You like me. You're what you are. I'm what I am. Life is like it is. Let's us go. An' if they's a little feelin' left over, then maybe when we're done you'll slip into my pocket just a little dough . . . okay? Shirt pocket. The one with the button. Button it, please. Don't be sad.

We ain't put here to make one another sad, down here below. That ain't what we're here for.

AEGIS *(After a pause).*

When you're ready. When you're ready, we'll go. I'll take you . . . wherever you want to go.

RAY

Aw, I'm ready. I been ready. Let's go.

(He stands and weaves just a bit)

Help me out.

*(*AEGIS *grabs him to steady him)*

Help me out an' we'll go wherever we got to go to. But mister—?

AEGIS

Aegis. The name is Aegis.

(Smiles)

Really.

RAY

Aegis. Mister Aegis. Okay. But make sure I stay drunk, okay? I do have to be drunk. Say that's okay. An' then we'll go.

AEGIS *(Finally).*

Okay.

RAY *(With a great smile).*

Okay.

(Drinks last of tequila)

Okay. We go.

(They exit, with AEGIS *helping maneuver* RAY *away through the rude frame door)*

END OF SCENE 1

S C E N E   T W O

The Time is several months later. The Setting is a first-class suite on a luxury liner. We could not be in a world more different from the tacky bar of Scene 1. Everything is muted mauve fabric and sensuous dark-brown woodwork, with subtle Deco aluminum decoration.

RAY, clad in becoming silk underwear, sits on the edge of a bed, drinking from a bottle of expensive whiskey. The bed is considerably rumpled. On the second bed, which is quite neatly made, there is a pile of men's clothes. It is evening.

RAY *(Sings).*
I'm crossin' over that River Jordan.
I'm crossin' back to my rotten ol' home.
I'm crossin' over that Atlantic Ocean—
    (AEGIS enters from the bathroom in an elegant floor-length robe, drying his hair. He leans in the doorway, gazing fondly at RAY. RAY notices him and raises the bottle in a friendly toast.)
Unless ol' Aegis once more decides to roam.
    (RAY speaks)
Farewell, ol' Europe. You was—
    (Corrects himself)
—were—fun while you lasted.

AEGIS
Do you want to get dressed and go up on deck?

RAY
Sure. That'd be nice. Is they—is there a moon?

AEGIS *(Wanders about stateroom, drying himself).*
Well, there was a full one last night, so there's a fair chance there will be one tonight, yes.

RAY
Ah, boy, that was fine last night, wasn't it? I think people oughta have a costume ball ev'ry night o' their lives. You was—were— real dashin' in that red devil outfit.

AEGIS

You looked pretty dashing in that Swiss Guards costume, yourself.

RAY

Whyn't we put 'em back on an' go up on deck?

AEGIS *(Seats himself on other bed)*.

It isn't done.

RAY

Ain't that—isn't that—funny? One night it's okay to dress any way you want to, an' the next night it'd shock ever'body silly. Isn't that funny?

AEGIS *(Enjoying* RAY *immensely)*.

You could get into that sleek new tuxedo, and we could go up to the midnight musicale.

RAY

Mmmmm. That'd be nice. For the very last night of our trip.

(Toasts AEGIS, *drinks)*

I sure do like that tuxedo.

AEGIS *(Pleasantly, not pushing)*.

Or we could stay here?

RAY

Okay. Will you put on your red devil costume?

AEGIS

If you'd like me to.

RAY

Might be fun.

AEGIS

We should have gotten you an angel suit.

RAY

Ha! That'd be nice.

AEGIS

Or a jester's outfit.

RAY

What's jester?

AEGIS

Yellow and black tights and a cap with bells. Like that Chinese dancer wore at the Folies Bergere.

RAY

Now, wasn't he good? Or I could wear nothin' but a bunch o' bananas, like that nigra gal wore.

(He stands and does a comic bump-and-grind, and falls onto his bed happily laughing)

AEGIS

Who *are* you?

RAY

Someone real happy. An' hopes you are, too. Wanna drink?

(Extends bottle)

AEGIS *(With a fleeting frown of concern).*

No . . . thanks.

RAY *(Takes a long swig).*

Tomorra mornin'll we really see New York again?

AEGIS

Yes. The New World awaits us.

RAY

It ain't the New World. It's the old one. Yurp was the New World. Sorry, Eu-rope. Two syllables.

AEGIS *(Carefully).*

Ray . . . we could spend a few days in New York, if you'd like.

RAY *(Beaming).*

Oh, yeah.

AEGIS

There's so much I'd like to show you in New York.

RAY

Tell me about it?

AEGIS

Well, New York is different than—

RAY *(Correcting* AEGIS*)*

Different from.

AEGIS *(Smiles).*

Different from any city in the whole world. It has more energy, more saloons, more salons, more beggars, more millionaires, more shows, more sights, more secrets, more museums and churches—

RAY

More people like you?

AEGIS

Yes, I'm sure. Well, maybe not more of any one thing than some other cities, but more of all of them put together than any city you've ever been in.

RAY

Seventeen.

AEGIS

What?

RAY *(Proudly).*

Seventeen cities I been in in my life now.

AEGIS

Is it seventeen?

RAY *(Sits up and counts on his fingers, switching bottle back and forth).*

Plainsville. Fort Worth. Saint Louis. Chicago. New York. London. Amsterdam. Antwerp. Vienna. Paris. Bruges. Char-truh. Rheims. Brussels. Madrid. Liverpool. London.

AEGIS

You named London twice.

RAY

It was like a diff'rent city the second time.

AEGIS

I was afraid to show you all of it the first time through.

RAY

Afraid why?

AEGIS

I . . . wasn't sure how much you'd want to see. I didn't know how interested you were in . . . all kinds of things.

RAY *(Kneels before* AEGIS, *casually).*

I have liked ever'thing we seen—saw. I never dreamed they— there—was so much to see. There . . . hasn't . . . been a day or night when you . . . haven't . . . showed me . . . shown me . . . somethin' new an' wonderful an' beautiful an' excitin'.

AEGIS

I wasn't sure about that show in Soho.

RAY

Shit, Aegis. There isn't nothin' mean nor ugly nor dirty that you showed me that was new to me. I . . . knew . . . all them things before. Those things. But all the nice things, they was new—were new. I'll thank you to my dyin' day for ever'thing we . . . saw . . . together.

AEGIS

And now you're going to let me show you New York?

RAY

Let you? I will never—won't never understand you.

AEGIS

Well, I'd like to make this trip last a little longer.

RAY *(Rises, walks away, stands with his back to* AEGIS*).*

I wisht I understood what I did—done—did that was wrong.

AEGIS

You? Nothing. Why do you say that?

RAY

I been dyin' to see New York. I liked what I saw of it before we sailed. It looked wonderful. I can't think of . . . anything . . . nicer than stayin' there.

AEGIS

I'm very glad to hear you say that, Ray.

RAY

I been tryin' to be well-behaved an' learn how to act with people in ever' place you took me. I'm tryin' to talk better an' pay attention about art an' history an' all. I sure hope I ain't embarrassed you none nor made you sorry none that you tooken—took—me with you.

AEGIS *(Rises).*

No, Ray, never. I hope I haven't given you that impression.

RAY *(Beginning to cry).*

If they . . . there . . . is anything I ain't been doin' that you want me to do, or somethin' I been doin' wrong, or not doin' enough of, I would be glad if you would tell me so I can change my ways. I'm willin' to work hard an' learn to please you in ever' way I can, but you got to *tell* me, 'cause all this is new to me, an' I ain't like you, so I can't guess what it is to do an' what not to do. If I'm not makin' good, you got to tell me.

AEGIS *(Upset and puzzled).*

Ray, what have I done or said to make you carry on this way? What can I do to tell you what these last few months have been for me? You've taken the whole world and shaken it out so that the dust fell away, and it's all like new again. You've made me see things in myself I had put away since childhood. You've shown me a tenderness I had forgotten I ever dreamed of.

RAY

Well, then, what do you want to make me go an' cry for, tellin' me I have to go away, an' teasin' me about how we only get to stay in New York for a few days? Aegis, please, why are you tryin' to get rid of me?

AEGIS *(Shocked, uncertain what to do or say).*

Ray, I just ... assumed you'd want to get back to your wife and children.

RAY

Oh, what for? What you been givin' 'em is more'n they ever seen before. An' it ain't puttin' you out none, is it?

AEGIS

No, it's negligible.

RAY

Well, see? God, why would anybody wanna go back there for? It's filthy an' ugly an' poor an' I ain't thought about it, 'cept when I have nightmares, not wunst since we went away from it. God, ever'where we been they's been things so nice an' so pretty. An' bein' with you is so nice an' so fun. An' now New York?

(Earnestly, hardly aware that he is crying)

I'll do anything you want me to to stay with you in New York. If it's the sleepin' together, I mean if you're tired o' that, I'll be glad to stay on an' do anything else. That place back there, it ain't got nothin' I want to go back to. If they's any way I can stay with you, if they's any other work I can do for you, please, please, please, tell me how.

AEGIS *(Longing to embrace* RAY*).*

Ray, my God, there's nothing in the universe I'd rather do than stay with you in New York, forever. If I haven't asked you, it's because ... Ray, I never thought you'd want to be with me longer than just a ... trip. I haven't ever asked about your feelings because ... well, I suppose because I thought I knew them. I suppose I didn't want to hear you say ... what I thought you'd say. I want to stay with you. I want you to stay with me. Don't you know my feelings, either?

RAY *(Beginning to smile through his failing tears).*

Well, no, o' course I don't. How could I? I don't never hope to understand people like you. But I ain't guessed wrong what to do anywheres, have I? Even in Brussels an' Bruges? An' New York's better, ain't—isn't it? I mean, back in Plainview, we'd be likely to have a little trouble, wouldn't we? I mean the way things is—are —between us?

AEGIS

Yes. Yes, we would.

RAY *(Growing ever happier).*

But in New York, it won't be so bad, will it? I mean, if it's anything like London an' Amsterdam, they's—there's—plenty of you people there, ain't they? Aren't there? We could be pretty much let alone?

AEGIS

Pretty much.

RAY

An' there, if you ever get tired o' me, they's probably other men in New York like you that might like me, wouldn't they be? You probably got friends like you there? That might be willin' to take me on for somethin'?

AEGIS *(Shocked, stunned, disbelieving).*

Yes. Yes, of course, I have friends there. But, Ray, you never need to worry about that happening.

RAY *(Blissfully happy, unaware of* AEGIS*'s torment).*

Aw, thank you, Aegis. God, I'm so glad we got to talk. I been so tense, wonderin' when you was gonna make me go back. Aw, God, it's good to have that off my back.

(Takes a quick swig)

I been wantin' to cry before now, if you want to know.

AEGIS

No. No, I don't want to know that you ever want to cry.

RAY

Aw, good.

(He is pacing about happily)

Then all you have to do is let me stay. An' keep me a little drunk, of course.

AEGIS

Of course.

RAY

You'll tell 'em that, won't cha? If they's somebody else that you decide to give me to? That I do have to be kept a little drunk? 'Cause they oughta know. It wouldn't be fair to ask 'em to take me on without them knowin' that. 'Cause I know it's a certain amount o' extra expense, an' I wouldn't want it to come as a surprise to no one.

AEGIS *(Staring at the sweet, sad actuality of love).*

Yes, yes. I'll tell them. If that should ever happen, Ray.

RAY *(With a great sigh of relief).*

Aw, good!

(Starts to drink, finds bottle empty)

Hey, hand me that other bottle, won't cha?

(AEGIS does. RAY opens it as he speaks)

Now! An' do you wanna go out in our tuxedoes, like you said? Or stay in an' play in our costumes? Or what do you wanna do?

AEGIS *(Sits on his bed).*

I want ... to lie here and look at you for a long while, and think about you.

(He stretches out on his bed)

RAY

Okay. An' what do you want me to do?

(Takes a drink)

AEGIS

Whatever you want to do, Ray.

RAY

Okay!

(Toasts AEGIS *and lies down on his own bed, a happy man)*

I just wanna lie here an' be real happy, happy like I ain't—haven't—never—ever—been before. An' you just tell me if they's—there's—anything at all that you want me to do.

*(*RAY *sings to the ceiling as* AEGIS *lies propped up on one elbow, looking at him)*

I'm crossin' over that River Jordan.
I'm crossin' over to my heavenly home.
I'm crossin' over that River Jordan,
Nevermore to ramble, nevermore to roam.

C U R T A I N

1 9 4 0 s

▭▪▭

BILL BATCHELOR
ROAD

for my sisters

BILL BATCHELOR

ROAD

The setting is the patio-terrace of BOB's *and* BILL's *home in Honeydew, California. How to describe this home?* BOB *built it himself to fulfill the wildest dreams of a dust-bowl Okie, who saw a lot of movies. It has Gothic turrets, Venetian arcades, brightly enameled Pennsylvania Dutch kitchen doors, Moorish tile floors depicting scenes from desert films, and brown-and-white Tudor walls. All of this is punctuated with a general aura of mud-colored, thick-troweled stucco and brick-red roof tiles in the style known, and loved, as California Spanish.*

This particular patio-terrace is graced with trees, vines, flowers, and shrubs planted by BILL *when* BOB *got through.*

The time is April of 1945, a bright spring morning. BOB BOSEMAN, *a rangy, laconic man in his forties, sits at a breakfast table in the sunshine, sipping at coffee and toying with remnants of toast, as he browses through a newspaper.* BOB *wears a state trooper uniform complete with shoulder holster and gun. A voice calls from within the house.*

BILL *(Inside).*
Bob? Bob, sugar?

BOB *(Calls without looking up from his paper).*
Out here on the patio-terrace still dawdlin' over breakfast, Bill, honey.

(BILL enters with a plate of toast and a Silex coffeepot. As he speaks, he busies himself pouring coffee, clearing dishes, etc. BILL is a cut above BOB in education and wears a Western shirt and jeans covered by a flowered kitchen apron)

BILL

It said just now on my kitchen radio that that Mister Truman is going to have to be the President now, Bob.

BOB

Well, that should be good, Bill. I believe he used to be a school-teacher like you are.

BILL

I wonder why it is that we don't ever get to have our President from here in California.

BOB

Americans don't understand Californians.

BILL

Well, all that to one side, Bob, wherever are we finally going to put that darned hummingbird bath?

BOB *(Pauses with coffee cup halfway up and lays paper down carefully).*

Well, I'm sure that I don't know, Bill. Just whereabouts would you think?

BILL

Well, if we were to put it here on the patio-terrace, we could then sit by and watch them use it.

BOB

Well ... but do we know it for a fact that they're goin' to come here to the patio-terrace to use it?

BILL

Well, no. But they come here to get fed, and so I imagine it is safe to assume that they would come to bathe as well.

BOB

Well ... but maybe they is some kinds of birds that don't like to bathe too near to where they eat.

BILL *(Scattering toast-crumbs for birds).*

Do you, personally, know of any such birds?

BOB

I cannot say that I do, no.

BILL

Well, can you think of any other place where we could put it that they would be more likely to come to use it?

BOB

Now, I didn't say that they would *not* come to the patio-terrace to use it. I only wondered aloud as to if you knew whether they would come or they would not.

BILL

Well, with your apparent encyclopediac knowledge of humming-birds, is there any reason that you can think of that they would not?

BOB

Well, no, not unless they was cats here that they would be afraid of.

BILL

Well, there have never been any cats here so far.

BOB

Well, but I was just answerin' what it was you asked.

BILL

Well, and I think I answered what you answered, so my question still is: do you think that the patio-terrace is a good place to erect it or do you think that there is some other area that might prove to be more advantageous to put it in some way or another in the long run?

BOB

Well . . .

BILL *(Grabs a broom and begins sweeping up).*

Take your time. We have done without a hummingbird bath this long; I imagine we can do without one until you decide where you want it.

BOB

Now, they is no particular place where I would want it more than any another, Bill. Honey. Anywhere that you desire to put it will be all right with me. I feel that a hummin'bird bath will be a attractive addition to the beauty and value of the house wherever you choose to put it, so I am relatively indifferent to its placement, all things concerned.

BILL

Is that your last word on it?

BOB

Well, yes.

BILL

Fine. I have placed cementing materials over there on the other side of this patio-terrace for it, so just as soon as you finally finish breakfast, you can go ahead and begin installing it there.

BOB

Oh. Well. All right.

BILL

I *had* thought that around back in the lanai among my hibiscus would be a dramatic situation for it, but I guess since the birds are accustomed to coming to this patio-terrace, this is as good a place as any other would be.

BOB

Well, now, wait a minute, Bill. If you don't want it on the patio-terrace, then I have no wish to go against your wishes regardin' what will, after all, be a fairly permanent fixture—

BILL

And involving a lot of cementing work.

BOB

That is a consideration, I admit. But if you wish it to be around in back instead of than in this patio, or if you are as yet undecided, then I am more than willin' to delay the installation—

BILL

And a few hours of honest work.

BOB

—until such time as you are clear in your mind about any doubts as to and concernin' its more preferable location.

BILL

No, no, I don't see any reason to dawdle anymore. We've been talking about putting it in since Roosevelt's first term, and I can easily picture us talking about it until the end of recorded time if we don't finally get it set into its place this spring!

BOB

Well, I fail to see the reason for the sudden rush, as I bought it for you over my own objections as to what the neighbors, when we get any, might think of two grown men havin' a hummin'bird bath some years before you started to lose your hair, and you have never seen fit to get a place picked out for it the hundred or so times that I have politely asked you whether you knew where you wanted the golly-darned damned thing put!

BILL

Please. The last thing in the world I would want is for us to in any way disagree. Put it wherever and whenever you want it put and that will be quite all right with me. Do you want some more eggs or some more coffee?

BOB

Well, can't I have both?

BILL

You can have anything you want, sugar, if you will plant that beloved birdbath somewhere where I won't have to trip over it every time I go to get out the lawn mower!

(With sudden dignity)

I got some mango jam I haven't told you about. I'll go get it now while you fume.

(BILL exits)

BOB *(Calls)*.

I find myself somewhat at a loss to understand why you are bein' so difficult and unmanageable about a stone-age issue like that birdbath on this particularly joyous sunbathed mornin' of all times!

BILL *(Re-enters with jam)*.

I do not consider that I am being unmanageable or—

BOB

—difficult—

BILL

—difficult about anything. And here is your mango jam.

(Sets it down, almost weeping)

Which I happen to know is a particular favorite of yours.

BOB *(Touched)*.

Aw, honey, now what *is* the matter with you? Aw, did some one more of them poor sweet service boys that we know die?

(He embraces BILL)

BILL *(Produces telegram from apron pocket)*.

Yes. That pretty little Howie Lawson from Western Virginia caught himself one in the Aleutians. I received a telegram from the War Department this mornin'.

BOB

Aw, Howie had 'em send us a telegram?

BILL

Yes. For some reason he had it addressed to Mrs. Bill Batchelor, so I was at first reluctant to accept it for your fear of causing talk. Then I decided that it would pass for an error on the part of a telegraphic device, and I took it and tipped the old deliveryman a quarter.

BOB

I imagine Howie had to give a invented reason for includin' us amongst those to be notified in the case of his passin'.

BILL

Well, for whatever reason, that is how it came. And here it is.

BOB

Aw, poor little Howie.

BILL

So I just thought that to put the hummingbird bath up at this specific moment would make it serve as something of a monument to the memory of Howie, remembering what particular regard he always held for the hummingbirds, as well as a convenience for the birds themselves, and a means of drawing them here where they tend to look so attractive among the olive trees.

BOB

I agree wholeheartedly with you, Bill, and I will certainly make sure that I have completed at least all *preparatory* work upon it before I must go out on my highway patrol.

BILL

Thank you. I think Howie would have liked it.

BOB

Are you goin' to put his telegram in your scrapbook?

BILL

Yes, I wanted to show it to you before I did.

BOB

And get me to put in the birdbath.

BILL

I can put in a birdbath myself, Bob. I thought I would give you the opportunity to do so before I went ahead with it.

BOB

You could have put it in yourself in the time we been talkin' about it.

BILL

I could have built the Great Wall of China in the time we've been talking about it.

BOB

Bill, do you want for us to fight?

BILL

No ...

BOB

Well, then, what is it that you wish for us to do?

BILL

Well ... do you absolutely have to go out on patrol today?
(He toys with BOB's *gun)*

BOB

Well ...
(Checks his wristwatch)
Yes.

BILL *(Sultry).*

Well, be home in time for lunch, then. We'll paste the telegram in the scrapbook and ...
(With a languorous look)
... take a nap.

BOB

All right, honey. I'll finish my coffee and get to work, then.

BILL *(Points across terrace).*

You'll find everything you need right there.

BOB *(Tightening the embrace).*

Not quite ever'thing, honey.

BILL

Don't start anything you don't have time to finish. I have some papers to grade.

(An elaborate door chime rings. BILL *breaks away)*

There is somebody at our door. I'll get it while you start.

*(*BILL *starts toward door)*

BOB

Please take off your apron. They is no tellin' who it might be.

*(*BOB *sits at table)*

BILL *(Halts).*

After fifteen years, Bob, my apron comes off by automatic reflex.

BOB

What about the time the P.T.A. chairlady come by with them leaflets?

BILL *(As he divests himself of the apron).*

I explained to her convincingly about wartime shortages of materials, and I never want to hear the word "leaflets" again!

*(*BILL *flings the apron across the patio into* BOB*'s face and exits huffily to answer the door)*

BOB *(Hanging apron neatly over* BILL*'s chair).*

Maybe it would be best to just sit here and contemplate some design plans over coffee before I commence the actual irreversible work of the installation.

(And he pours himself the last of the coffee and exits for more)

BILL *(Offstage).*

Hello?

REVEREND LAWSON *(Offstage)*.

How do you do? I am looking for Mrs. Bill Batchelor?

BILL *(Offstage)*.

Oh, no, not another one!

REVEREND LAWSON *(Offstage)*.

I beg your pardon?

BILL *(Offstage)*.

I'm sorry. It has been a very bad morning. Just let me have it, and here is a quarter for you.

REVEREND LAWSON *(Offstage)*.

I'm sorry. I am not blessed to know what you are talking about. I am the Reverend Howard Lawson from Walking, West Virginia. I was given this address for Mrs. Bill Batchelor. Is this her address?

BILL *(Offstage)*.

Well, it is and it isn't. You had better follow me out to the patio-terrace.

(BILL re-enters from one side just as BOB re-enters from the other)

BOB

What is it, Bill?

BILL

It's a gentleman that says he is Reverend. Take your holster off.

BOB *(Does so and hangs it on his chair)*.

Oh . . . well . . . all right.

(The REVEREND LAWSON, a saintly cadaver in full pastor's regalia, enters and stands blinking in the sun)

BOB

Well, do come in, Reverend.

REVEREND LAWSON

Oh. Yes. Excuse me. I had thought I was coming indoors.

BILL

It's a patio-terrace, Reverend. This is Mister Bob Boseman. Bob, Reverend Howard *Lawson*.

REVEREND LAWSON *(Advances, shakes hands with* BOB*)*.

I'm pleased to meet you. You are a police officer?

BOB

I am a state trooper, Reverend . . .

(Turns to BILL*)*

. . . Lawson?

BILL

Howard Lawson.

REVEREND LAWSON

Is there some trouble here?

BOB

Not none nothin' can be done about. Bill, do you have any more coffee left?

BILL

I do, yes.

BOB

I mean for the Reverend Lawson.

BILL

Well, yes, of course, if he should want any.

BOB

Do you want some coffee, Reverend Lawson?

REVEREND LAWSON

Certainly. Thank you. That would be very nice.

BILL

Do you want for me to go and get this coffee that the Reverend Lawson wants?

BOB

That had been my assumption, yes.

BILL

Thank you. I just like to be told these things.

(BILL *exits*)

BOB

Well, and so I presume you are the father of our former young friend, Howie Lawson.

REVEREND LAWSON

I was, Officer Boseman, before his passing.

BOB

Well, Reverend Lawson, and where have you come to us from?

REVEREND LAWSON

All the way from West Virginia. I have come to talk with Mrs. Bill Batchelor. I wonder if I have come to the right place?

BOB

Well, yes and no. How did you come?

REVEREND LAWSON

I drove, Officer Boseman.

BOB

You might as well call me Bob.

REVEREND LAWSON

Thank you, Bob.

BOB

That must have been expensive drivin' all this way to Southern California from the Western of Virginia, Reverend.

REVEREND LAWSON

Elderly parishoners who revered the memory of my and my wife Constance's deceased son, Howie, supplied me with scarce tires and plentiful gas-rationing coupons and their prayers, Bob. Is Mrs. Batchelor here?

BOB

Well, they ain't no Mrs. Batchelor, the way it has worked out.

REVEREND LAWSON

Oh, has there been an accident?

BOB

I'll say.

REVEREND LAWSON

Has Mrs. Batchelor been involved in a collision?

BOB

Oh, probably you think that because of my uniform here. I live here, Reverend Lawson. My presence don't indicate no incident, so you can relax about that, at least.

REVEREND LAWSON

I am somewhat confused. The gentleman at the Shell Station gave me directions to Bill Batchelor Road?

BOB

Yep. I named it that. I am the founder of this town of Honeydew, and so far Mister Batchelor and I are its only residents.

REVEREND LAWSON

I fail in understanding.

(BILL *re-enters with a tray bearing coffee things. Under his arm is a fat scrapbook*)

BILL

Here is Reverend Lawson's coffee. I am sorry for my brusqueness a few moments ago, Reverend Lawson, but the news of Howie's death had upset my characteristics. I am better now. There is cream and sugar here, or honey, preferred by some of us Californians for supposed reasons of health. Do sit.

(*They all sit*)

REVEREND LAWSON *(To* BILL*)*.

You, too, knew my and my wife Constance's son, Howie?

BILL

I did, and the news of his death about burnt my beans!

BOB

Bill!

BILL

Well, I'm sorry, but it did.

REVEREND LAWSON

You received your telegram only this morning?

BILL

Yes. That is why I was so distraught before.

REVEREND LAWSON

I see. You see, I and my wife Constance received our sad tidings a month ago.

BOB

Mail delivery in these parts is plumb medieval. Uh . . . what else is that you have got with you there, Bill?

BILL *(With a glare at* BOB*)*.

I have with me here our scrapbook for the relevant dates.

BOB

Have you indeed, Bill?

BILL

Indeed I have, Bob.

REVEREND LAWSON

I fear I must throw myself more or less on your mercies. When I and my wife Constance received our son Howie's hallowed remains, we also received a letter from him advising me and my wife Constance that his last and happiest days had been spent on a Bill Batchelor Road, and that should a Mrs. Bill Batchelor contact us, she was to be treated with the reverence and respect usually accorded only intimate family members. When such contact did not occur, it became an *idée fixe* with my wife Constance that we should locate this personage and acquire knowledge of her and my son Howie's last days. All normal means of inquiry proved futile, and, at last, under the pressure of my wife Constance, I undertook the journey here, owing, Bill, to generous bedridden parishoners. Upon arriving in this sweltering climate, I again met utter blankness until, by chance, I learned that the town of Honeydew, newly formed, contained a Bill Batchelor Road. And that is how I came here on this strange morning to be greeted by the news that the party I seek is a fiction?

BILL

Your boy was forced to a harmless subterfuge, owin' to the War Department's reluctance to part with a three-cent stamp to notify any but immediate family of military personnel meeting their mortality. It's a shame what circumambulations bureaucracy forces our boys to.

REVEREND LAWSON

So you are Mrs. Bill Batchelor, as it were?

BILL

Not really. I am Bill Batchelor.

REVEREND LAWSON

And my and my wife Constance's son Howie spent his last leave here with you? In this curious house?

BOB

Yes, and a sweeter boy never lived. Nor died.

BILL

Howie just loved it here. Bob built this house himself out of natural native stone and cement.

BOB

It has every feature in it that I ever wanted in a house.

BILL

Except possibly a birdbath.

REVEREND LAWSON

It is unique in my experience. I have not heretofore encountered Spanish Colonial pagodas. You will understand if I am somewhat distracted from appreciating it by anxiety for news of my and my wife Constance's—

BILL *(Interrupting)*.

Oh, surely. Here is the telegram which I received this morning. I will subsequently place it in this scrapbook along with the many others we have received about boys who enjoyed our home before departing to become deceased in the current conflict.

REVEREND LAWSON

You make a practice of offering entertainment to our brave boys before they go to do their duty?

BILL

If you want to put it that way. Here is a picture of Howie.

(He starts to offer REVEREND LAWSON *open scrapbook)*

BOB *(Timorous)*.

Uh ... I wonder what picture that is, Bill?

BILL

Just him doing his hula, Bob.

(Hands scrapbook to REVEREND*)*

REVEREND LAWSON *(Looking at picture)*.

This ... this is my and my wife Constance's—?

BOB

Yep, that's Howie. I'd know them stomach muscles anywhere.

REVEREND LAWSON

Howie worked out.

BOB

Howie worked out fine.

REVEREND LAWSON

What exactly is he doing on that table?

BILL

His hula.

REVEREND LAWSON

My and my wife Constance's son Howie learned the hula from some other young serviceman who had served a tour of duty in the South Seas?

BILL

I think he more picked it up at the movies.

BOB

Wherever he learnt it, it was a crowd pleaser.

BILL

Remember that marine?

BOB

Oh, Arnold.

BILL

He like to left us for another sphere of existence when Howie began his routine.

REVEREND LAWSON

What is that obscuring my and my wife Constance's son Howie's face?

BOB

One of Bill's hibiscuses.

REVEREND LAWSON

And these other young men around the table. There was a party?

BILL

Night and day.

BOB

Oh, we always had a few in residence.

BILL

That's Arnold there. He like to slit a wrist when Howie had to go.

REVEREND LAWSON

My and my wife Constance's son Howie had a special friend among your young charges here?

BOB *(Points at picture)*.

Yes, Arnold, that one there.

REVEREND LAWSON

This was a costume party?

BOB

Started out that way, but then Arnold got to where we couldn't get him out o' that caveman outfit night nor day.

BILL

Here's a photo of Arnold up in our jacaranda tree.

REVEREND LAWSON

Good heavens, that poor boy. He must have been so embarrassed.

BOB

What by?

REVEREND LAWSON

That angle reveals his manhood.

BILL

It's in shadow, though.

REVEREND LAWSON

I suppose in the rush of wartime help shortages, such things slipped by the developer's eye.

BOB

They don't a lot slip by ol' Georgie Carter, over to the Kodak shop.

REVEREND LAWSON *(Indicating photo of Arnold).*

I should like to meet this young man.

BILL

Who wouldn't?

REVEREND LAWSON

He might perhaps have recollections, personal memories of my and my wife Constance's—

BOB & BILL

Son Howie.

BOB

Yes, he would of, 'ceptin' he died on Guadalcanal.

REVEREND LAWSON

Oh, how unfortunate.

BOB

To put it mildly.

BILL

Yes, there's his telegram, see?

REVEREND LAWSON

And these others?

BOB

Them is from other boys we have known that have got themselves killed in this continuin' war.

REVEREND LAWSON

What wonderful selfless work our home-front folks have done in this war. I and my wife Constance have frequently dispensed doughnuts. Has anyone, I wonder, written up what you men do?

BILL

That Mister Isherwood intended to.

BOB

I talked him out of it, though.

REVEREND LAWSON

All these wires! You have undergone so many losses?

BOB

Yep. It gets to be almost routine.

BILL *(Kicks* BOB *under the table).*

No it doesn't.

BOB

No, of course it don't.

REVEREND LAWSON

We must comfort ourselves with the realization that it is all part of God's great plan.

BILL *(With a decisive tone).*

Oh, must we now?

BOB

Bill . . .

REVEREND LAWSON

Yes, all is for the best. I wonder, might I have a copy made of this photo of my and my wife Constance's—

BILL

Reverend Lawson, wouldn't you rather have one where there is nothing obscuring his face?

REVEREND LAWSON

Why, yes. To be perfectly frank, just between us fellows, I'm not really sure my wife Constance would—

BILL *(Grabbing scrapbook away and leafing through).*

Let me just look. I do believe there's another photo here of your and your wife Constance's—

BOB *(Trying to take scrapbook).*

Oh, no, I don't believe they is, Bill—

BILL *(Holding onto scrapbook).*

Oh, yes, there is, Bob.

(Stamps on BOB's *foot.* BOB *lets go.* BILL *continues to search through scrapbook)*

REVEREND LAWSON

How did you come, may I ask, to encounter my and my—

BOB

Oh, I run into him doin' my rounds of the bus station over to Los An-gee-leez.

REVEREND LAWSON

You patrol clear into Los Angeles?

BOB

Not officially, no.

BILL *(Finds picture).*

Ah, here he is. That's a stunning picture of Howie.

REVEREND LAWSON

Oh, do let me see.

BOB *(Pleading).*

Honey . . .

REVEREND LAWSON *(Misunderstanding "Honey").*

No, thank you, I prefer sugar. Oh, this will mean so much to—

(Gapes at picture, his voice rising)

MY WIFE CONSTANCE!

BILL

I think that's where I'll put the telegram.

BOB

Sigh. I guess Howie would have wanted it this way.

REVEREND LAWSON *(Pointing at picture)*.

What is this?

BOB

You and your wife Constance's son Howie.

REVEREND LAWSON

But what is *this*?

BILL

You and your wife Constance's son Howie's ass.

BOB

And a hibiscus.

REVEREND LAWSON

What is the meaning of this?

BILL

He said nobody had ever taken him a picture of that, so I obliged him.

REVEREND LAWSON

All of these are pictures of young men naked!

BOB *(Critically)*.

Except for high black socks.

BILL

Bob, don't start.

BOB

I think that's so unhealthy.

BILL

Well, you like dogtags.

BOB

I don't *mind* dogtags. That's differ'nt.

BILL

Well, then don't get snide about my socks.

REVEREND LAWSON *(Turns a page)*.

Good God, what is this?

BILL

Those are Delmore Evans and Philip Eckerman.

BOB

An' most of Obie Mankiwiecz.

BILL

That's when you bought me the new stop-action device.

BOB

War brings many advances.

BILL

But at such an awful cost.

REVEREND LAWSON

Gentlemen, I must have an explanation of this.

BILL

Which one?

REVEREND LAWSON *(Stands)*.

This book, this anthology of filth.

BOB

Oh, sit down.

REVEREND LAWSON

You men are pornographers.

BOB

We are not, neither.

BILL
Yes, we are, too.

BOB
Well, not like he means.

REVEREND LAWSON
You made my son pose for this indecency.

BILL
He begged for it.

BOB
They all did.

BILL *(Riffling through scrapbook).*
Lads just love to pose for pictures of their things.

BOB
It seemed little enough to do for them.

BILL *(Locates picture).*
Here's one of Howie and his friend.

BOB
One of your best.

BILL
I'm pleased with it. See the little curly golden hairs on Arnold?

REVEREND LAWSON
Oh, my God, what are they doing?

BOB *(Glances at photo).*
Buttfuckin'.

BILL
Well, Arnold is.

BOB
Howie was partial to blondes.

BILL

But not fetishistical or anything.

BOB

No, but he liked blondes.

BILL

He liked that black boy from Dayton.

BOB

Well, he was one of the few that could take his and his wife Constance's son Howie.

BILL

Howie *was* huge.

REVEREND LAWSON

You men are homosexual.

BOB *(Correcting the* REVEREND*).*

Homosexuals.

REVEREND LAWSON

You forced my boy to engage in acts of homosexuality.

BILL

Oh, we did not.

REVEREND LAWSON

Are you saying that my and . . . that Howie was homosexual?

BILL

I always wondered about that.

BOB

I never thought he was, but I didn't want to hurt Arnold.

BILL

Arnold was so heartbroken.

BOB

I never thought Arnold was.

BILL

Heartbroken? Sure he was.

BOB

No, homosexual.

BILL

I don't think he was, but he wanted Howie to be.

BOB

Oh, I know.

BILL

He wanted Howie to have nothin' but blond men in memory of him.

BOB

Did Howie stick to that?

BILL

I don't think he ever wrote us about that.

REVEREND LAWSON

This entire book is nothing but young men doing homosexual things together.

BILL

Well, what else could they do together?

REVEREND LAWSON

You held my son here for his whole last leave?

BILL

They most of them stayed the whole time once they got here.

BOB

Wunst they'd seen Grauman's Chinese theater and a flamingo.

BILL

You always say that. They could see flamingos right near here at the movie bird farm.

BOB

I was speakin' figuratively.

BILL

You always say that, though. Reverend Lawson, they could see flamingos right near here if they wanted to.

REVEREND LAWSON

In this house, on this obscene patio-terrace, you forced my and my wife—

BOB *(Stands)*.

Reverend Lawson, you're gettin' way out of bounds.

BILL

Nobody forced Howie to do anything.

BOB

Well, in all honestly, honey, I don't think he wanted to do his first three-way.

BILL

He *said* that, but it got to be his favorite thing.

BOB

Until he met Arnold.

REVEREND LAWSON

You prattle like children when you have done this damnable thing. You must be insane!

BILL

And just a minute ago you were being so nice about us.

REVEREND LAWSON

I am going to expose you monsters to the press, to the police, to the church, to the government, and to . . . and to . . . and to . . .

BILL

Oh, you are not.

BOB

You want them pictures of your boy in all the papers?

BILL

With the best parts cut out?

BOB

Just sit down now, Reverend Lawson, an' don't have yourself a heart attack. It gets hot here.

REVEREND LAWSON

I have heard whispered rumors about you people. I have even preached veiled sermons about you. But to know that I am in the presence of such iniquity! Iniquity!

BOB

Now just one minute, Reverend.

REVEREND LAWSON

I'm going! I'm going right now!

BOB

You just go ahead and try. I'll have you locked up in ten minutes for speedin'.

(The REVEREND *halts, stymied)*

This is California, sir, the motor state, and don't nobody cross a state trooper.

REVEREND LAWSON

You use official corruption to protect your degradation?

BILL

Well, you have to use what you've got against you people.

BOB

This is a free country, Reverend Lawson, and we can do anything we want to do, and people like you have just got to get educated.

REVEREND LAWSON

To think that the last experience of those poor boys was—

BOB
Love and sex and friendship and romance and happiness.

BILL
Like it promises us in our Constitution.

BOB
No it don't.

BILL
Well, it should.

REVEREND LAWSON
You have corrupted enough young men to fill a scrapbook!

BOB
Oh, that's just one of . . . how many is it now, honey?

BILL
Forty-two, sugar.

REVEREND LAWSON
Hundreds! Hundreds of young men!

BILL
Yes, their hearty laughter used to ring in my Bob's hand-tiled halls.

BOB
An' comin' home from the grocery store an' shoutin', "All right, ever'body drop your cocks an' grab your socks!" An' they'd tumble out in their skivvies an' their T-shirts!

BILL
And Freddie McIntyre in that wedding dress he fancied.

BOB
An' they'd hoist the boxes off the truck an' bring 'em in an' we'd cut sandwiches.

BILL
And we'd sit up in the kitchen at all hours.

BOB

Simple fare, but they never complained.

BILL

They understood.

BOB

An' when Ruben Vasquelez was here, he'd play his guitar.

BILL

Oh, there was always one of them would play the guitar or the harmonica, or even that boy with the blue eyelids who was a real concert pianist!

BOB

Yes, most of 'em, wunst they'd got over their natural reserve in the general atmosphere of good-natured fun, had some little skit or song or dance which they enjoyed to do.

BILL

Oh, or we'd put on the phonograph and go out in the moonlight on the patio, and the scent of my lilacs would mingle with their shadows on all that white flesh, pink flesh, brown, red, black flesh movin' in couples to the strains of saxophones.

BOB

Tall brown boys in jockstraps would dance with sticky red boys, with leis made of your camellias crushed between 'em.

BILL

Or a skinny farm boy in nothin' but a flight cap would lean sadly against a wall sucking on a coke and jerking off.

BOB

And he never went single-handed long if you wasn't busy passin' out potato chips, honey.

BILL

And come morning the front room looked like snowdrifts with the sheets we tossed over them when they collapsed in twos and threes after making love 'til their sweet young bodies begged for rest.

BOB

And some of 'em'd crawl in with us an' snuggle an' talk about they families an' girls an' dogs.

BILL

And cry about how frightened they were of goin' to have their beautiful young bodies riddled with bullets and torn by shrapnel and strung out over barbed wire.

BOB

Why, before our Howie went off to drown in a cold salt storm, he said to me, "Uncle Bob, I wish we could just do this 'til we die. Then I'd feel like I was givin' my life for somethin' decent."

BILL

I can still see him and Arnold dancing to their favorite song.
(Sings)
Oh, baby, don't blame yourself
Or be feeling bad.
Someone swell like you
Never should be sad.

BOB *(Sings)*.

Angel, don't blame yourself
Or be mixed up and blue,
'Cause from here on out,
I'm mixed up with you.

BILL *(Sings)*.

I know it's terrible
What we've gone and done.

BOB *(Sings)*.

But it's not unbearable

BOB & BILL *(Sing)*.

But the battle can't be won by one.
Babushka,
Don't shame yourself
For what you've put me through,

'Cause I found out lately it takes two
To make somebody baby blue.

BOB *(Speaks).*

An' now so many of 'em gone.

BILL

They were so beautiful.

BOB

They should of stood in bed.

REVEREND LAWSON

You lured those boys in here and made filth of them!

BOB

We don't think human bodies is filth until they're corpses, Reverend Lawson!

BILL

We loved every inch of those boys.

BOB

Every chance we got!

BILL

And we sent them off to war, since they had to go, with every single surface of them—

BOB

Tinglin' with kisses an' love.

REVEREND LAWSON

God forgive you for your absolute unrepentance.

BOB

Fuck you.

BILL

And your wife Constance.

(BOB *and* BILL *kiss*)

BOB

They ain't nothin' to repent for, Reverend Lawson. Them boys died for life, liberty, and the pursuit of happiness, an' we mean to see that they did not die in vain.

BILL

We do not intend to let uneducated people like you make a lie of this wonderful country's promise.

BOB

People came here for religious freedom, and we worshipped those boys.

BILL

We have done nothing wrong.

BOB

We are good Americans.

BILL

And we have the law on our side.

BOB *(Pats his gun).*

So to speak.

REVEREND LAWSON

You took those boys and made filth of them, I say.

(Points at picture in book)

You took this beautiful young man and made this indecency.

BOB

Oh, which one do you like?

BILL

Oh, that's Gregory Pegler. You're right. He was beautiful.

BOB

He was in prison in the Philippines an' had his lungs ruined.

BILL

But he married that nurse's aide that he had in the Navy Hospital in Bethesda, Maryland, and they have a perfectly healthy baby boy. There's its picture.

REVEREND LAWSON

Even naked babies! It's not enough for you that you corrupt a perfect young specimen like this!

BOB

You can keep that picture of Gregory if it excites you, Reverend.

BILL

We have more.

BOB

See, it was ever'body's favorite an' all the queer boys wanted prints.

BOB

Gregory is proud to think men masturbated to his image—

BOB & BILL

From Greenland to Guam.

REVEREND LAWSON

Oh, infinite putrefaction.

BILL

Maybe it's not Gregory that excites him. Maybe it's the torn khakis.

BOB

Is that it, Reverend Lawson? We understand about fetishism.

BILL

Jesse St. Clair wore those into action—

BOB

And got a Purple Heart on Corregidor.

REVEREND LAWSON

Oh, please, please, let me go from here. I can stand no more.

BILL

Yes, you do look like you might need to lie down for a while.

BOB

You shouldn't try a long drive back to Virginia in this condition.

BILL

Western Virginia, sugar.

BOB

Even Western Virginia, honey.

(*To* REVEREND LAWSON)

They's a nice room upstairs where we usually let the fathers sleep it off. And you can take Gregory's picture with you if you want to.

BILL

There are some more nice photos on the walls.

BOB

Is they any of your an' my an' his an' his wife Constance's boy Howie up there, honey?

BILL

There's a lovely one of Howie butterin' up Arnold in the bathtub.

BOB

The picture's in the bathtub?

BILL

No, the boys were, silly.

BOB

I see. Honey, I really got to get goin' on patrol. I promise I will do that birdbath in the mornin'. Now that we've met the Reverend, I do agree we should make a monument to our Howie.

BILL

Go keep our byways safe, sugar. I'll take care of the Reverend.

BOB

And should I still come back for our nap?

BILL

Oh, of course, sugar. Maybe we'll all take it together.

BOB

You never do know. Okay, I'll hurry. 'Bye honey.

(They kiss)

BILL

Bye. Oh, sugar?

BOB

What, Bill.

BILL

Do take your gun?

BOB

Right sugar.

*(*BOB *takes his gun and exits)*

*(*BILL *takes the* REVEREND LAWSON *slowly off. The* REVEREND *still clutches the picture of Gregory Pegler)*

BILL

There now. I'll take you upstairs and give you a sponge bath where our Howie bathed, and then you can just pass out. Or look at pictures if you like. We have so many. There were so many boys going off to kill and be killed. This old house was so full. I'm ashamed to say that in many ways it was a happy time. When Bob and I met years ago and realized how things were with us, we found this place for ourselves and built this house. It was Bob's idea to make this as yet unclaimed territory our own town. I named it Honeydew and he named its only thoroughfare for me. That was our way of showing that we were not going to let you poor unfortunate people make us unhappy. Then the war came and we found our mission, sending those boys off happy and fulfilled. Ah, those were happy times. And now we have our memories and our scrapbooks, and of course, there are the fathers to take care of. And, of course, we still have many happy times to come. Because now, after a war for freedom and liberty, all those boys will be coming back through. And we know they won't give up what they fought for. See, World War II veterans will be the most understanding generation ever. All those silly old taboos will be taken away, so all people can live happily under our American flag. Their sacrifices won't be wasted. See, all this hardship must have made people understand that love is good and we are good and that freedom must mean freedom for all if it is to mean anything. You can come upstairs and rest secure, Reverend Lawson. Our Howie went in a good cause. We can rest secure in a future of all-encompassing everlasting freedom. No, World War II will not have been fought in vain.

(BILL *leads the* REVEREND, *still clutching Gregory Pegler's picture, out of sight and away up them ol' stairs*)

C U R T A I N

1950s

ODD NUMBER

for Robert Luther Taylor

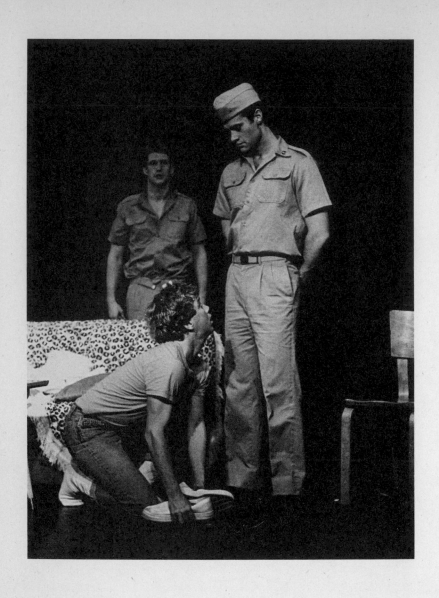

ODD NUMBER

The setting is the living room of a tract house in the town of Drinking Water, New Mexico.

Because it is the 1950s, there is, of course, a picture window. Were pink drapes not drawn across it, we would, of course, look through it into the picture window across the street. Since the drapes are drawn, we have instead the supernally beautiful glow of a New Mexico afternoon. As the play goes on, that glow becomes the throbbing deep red-golds of that state's unparalleled sunset.

All this magical light falls upon a brand-new living-room suite, advertised as "Swedish Modern." The two women who live here have good jobs, and in the world of post-war credit, have lots of worldly goods. The sofa has a nubby tan-and-brown plaid fabric; the walls bear framed knick-knack shelves with a mirrored background. They also support arte moderne plaques of Harlequin and Pierrot in unlikely beiges and turquoises. A long, low bookcase is filled principally with paperbacks, not Lesbian paperbacks; those are hidden in the bedroom. A similarly long, low coffee table made of polished slats features boomerang-shaped ashtrays in colors called chili and tamale.

At rise, it also holds a tray with a bottle of whiskey and two glasses, only one of which has been used. The couch is festooned with an Air Force Airman First Class uniform. The wall-to-wall carpet is partly hidden under a pair of blue jeans and a short-sleeved plaid shirt. Socks and shoes to match these outfits are scattered here and there. Two men, in brief, have undressed here in a hurry.

A record is playing on the "blond" stereo. It has been playing for some time. It is Doris Day's taffy-tone rendition of "Secret Love." There are doors that lead to a bathroom and a bedroom.

Out of the bedroom door comes airman BRAD KOWSKI, *a well-set-up young man draping a sheet around his nakedness. He stretches and yawns as if trying to get several kinks out of his slightly bruised body. The record ends, then starts to play again. He rushes to turn it off.*

BRAD *then flops down on the sofa, mightily exhausted. He notices the whiskey and pours himself a drink. Raising it to his lips, he smells his hand. He puts down the drink and smells both his hands, luxuriantly. He laughs, a laugh both joyous and desperate, and tosses his head like one trapped.*

A slyly beautiful seventeen-year-old boy named EDGAR *comes shyly into the bedroom doorway. He wears little white jockey shorts.*

EDGAR

Oh, hi. I thought maybe you had went back to the Air Force Base.

BRAD

Naw. Naw. I just got out of bed to get some rest.

(Chuckles)

EDGAR *(Gestures toward bedroom).*

You don't maybe want to come back in there?

BRAD

Not right now, honey, okay? Right now there's hamburger between these buns.

EDGAR *(Laughs and dares come forward).*

Ha! Is that what y'all say in New York?

(Starts to put on his T-shirt)

BRAD

Naw, that's somethin' I thought of just now.

(Downs drink)

Hey, don't do that.

EDGAR

Do what?

BRAD

Don't get dressed.

EDGAR

Oh. Well, I had thought maybe I had ought to.

BRAD

No, babe, don't ... I don't know if I got the strength to undress you again.

EDGAR *(Drops T-Shirt).*

Yeah. You know, nobody ever done that to me before.

BRAD

Did which?

EDGAR

Took my clothes off me. I didn't know people done that.

BRAD

You got to stop worryin' about what people do and don't do. Just ... do it and enjoy it. ... We ... do anything else you hadn't done before?

EDGAR

No. Well, I never done all of it with one guy before. And ...

BRAD

And what, baby? Tell me. I guess I got to know.

EDGAR *(A chuckle in his voice).*

And I never made so much *noise* doin' it before. Ain't it great Lena let us use her private home for it?

BRAD

Oh, God.

EDGAR

And I didn't dream people could do it so many times.

BRAD

Yeah. Yeah, that was a bit of a surprise. Where had you done it before?

EDGAR

Oh, you know, public places, like cars. I never done it where you could laugh and yell and talk about it before!

BRAD

Is that all that was new for you?

EDGAR

No ...

BRAD

Listen, baby, tell me. Don't be shy. Tell Brad.

EDGAR

That one thing ... you done ... so many times? You know, when you—

BRAD

Yeah, yeah, right, I know, you didn't have to tell me.

EDGAR

I didn't know—

BRAD

People did that. Gotcha.

EDGAR
Is it . . . all right to do?

BRAD
Jesus shit.

EDGAR
I mean—

BRAD
I know what you mean. Yes. It's all right.
(Long look between them)
Wasn't it?

EDGAR *(Throws himself into* BRAD*'s arms)*.
It was wunnerful!

BRAD
Do you want me to do it to you again?

EDGAR *(In heaven in his arms)*.
Uh-huh.

BRAD
Do you want to do it to me?

EDGAR
. . . I don't know.

BRAD
Tell me.

EDGAR
Maybe I ought to go?
(Rises)

BRAD *(Pulls him back, with no great resistance)*.
Tell me, Edgar. You don't have to go. Lena said we could use her
house 'til Monday. It's only Saturday evenin'. And your folks are
out of town.

EDGAR

I'm scared of you.

BRAD

Why? Because I do weird things?

(Releases EDGAR *and pours another drink)*

EDGAR

No. I just feel like you've got . . . some kind of . . . power over me.

BRAD

Jesus shit bricks.

(Gulps his drink)

EDGAR

I want to go, but when you ask me to stay, I get shaky.

BRAD

You're just wore out, that's all.

EDGAR

My heart's beating. I think I'm goin' to die.

(He places BRAD*'s hand on his breast)*

BRAD

No, you're not. So you're scared of me?

EDGAR

Uh-huh.

BRAD

You'll do anything I tell you?

EDGAR

Uh-huh.

(His voice is becoming shaky)

BRAD

Don't cry. You'll go down on me right here and now if I tell you
to?

EDGAR

Uh-huh.

BRAD

And you'll even do to me what I did to you?

EDGAR

If you tell me to.

BRAD

Stop crying. Answer me.

EDGAR

Yes! I'll do it to you!

BRAD

You'll do it to me right here in this living room? With me standing up and you on your knees? You'll do it to me for as long as I tell you to?

EDGAR

Yes, yes! I can't stop cryin'.

BRAD

And you'll let me take pictures of you doin' it?

EDGAR

If you want to. Oh, God, I'd do anything you told me to. I want to die.

BRAD

No, you don't. Come here, honey.

(They embrace on the sofa, tenderly)

EDGAR

I'm so happy. I'm so scared.

BRAD

I guess we're damn sure well and good queer, what do you think?

EDGAR

I don't care. I want to be with you. I want to die.

BRAD

Quit saying that. You dumb hillbilly.

EDGAR *(Laughs, gets up).*
I'm not a hillbilly.

BRAD

Anyone this side of the Hudson is a hillbilly.

EDGAR *(Putting on record out of a paper bag).*
This here is New Mexico. I am a clodhopper.

BRAD

You're a what?

EDGAR *(Turns on record, "Chances Are," by Johnny Mathis).*
A clodhopper, you dumb New Yorker. A farmer. Anyway, my grandpa was.

BRAD

You never saw a farm.

EDGAR *(Falling into BRAD's arms).*
No.
(They begin a monumental necking bee)
Is this all right? Just to hug and kiss like this?

BRAD

I'll tell you later.

EDGAR

All my life I watched boys and girls kiss while Johnny Mathis sang. All my life I wanted to do this like a real teenager.

BRAD

And what do you want to do now?

EDGAR

Oh, I could do this forever. I feel dizzy.

BRAD

Do you want to die anymore?

EDGAR

No. I want to live forever. Do you want me to do all those things you said? I will.

BRAD

I don't want you to do anything except what you're doin'. Don't you know what's happenin'?

EDGAR

Yes. I'm goin' to have a heart attack.

BRAD

No, you're not. Just go with it. Ride with it.

EDGAR

Oh, God, this is incredible.

BRAD

You're so dumb.

EDGAR

I'm not so dumb as you are. I know there's no way you could turn around and take a picture while I was doin' that thing you was goin' to make me do to you.

BRAD *(As the necking grows fast and furious).*

I don't want to make you do anything.

EDGAR

Lie!

BRAD

I want to make you do everything.

EDGAR
Yes, yes!

BRAD *(Shoves* EDGAR *away, stumbles over in his sheet and cuts off record).*
You silly hick. You don't know what's goin' on at all.
(Dives back to sofa, kisses EDGAR's *armpit)*

EDGAR *(Giggles voluptuously).*
How can you like *armpits?*

BRAD *(Suddenly solemn).*
Because they're your armpits.

EDGAR
What do you mean?

BRAD *(Trying to make a serious declaration).*
That crazy thing you wanted me to make you do to me?

EDGAR
Yes. Are you goin' to?

BRAD
I never did that to anyone before.

EDGAR
You didn't?

BRAD
Couldn't you tell I wasn't any good at it?

EDGAR
God! You mean it can be better?

BRAD
I'll show you real soon—

EDGAR
Oh, God, yes, yes, yes.

BRAD

—if you'll just let a man finish what I'm tryin' to say! . . . I let guys do that to me a couple of times. It made me feel superior and tough. But I never thought I'd do it to anyone.

EDGAR

Then why did you do it to me?

BRAD

Because I wanted to, dimwit. Because I had to.

EDGAR

Oh, God.

BRAD

From the minute I saw you in that record store, it was all I could think of. I couldn't believe myself. I looked at you in those stupid blue jeans, and I got this absolute—Technicolor!—picture of what was inside 'em. If you hadn't of gone into that stupid record booth, I would have dragged you into a parked car.

EDGAR

I thought I would die when you just . . . stopped that door and come right into the booth with me.

BRAD

I thought I'd die if I had to listen to that goopy record one more time.

EDGAR

I couldn't think of nothin' else to do to keep you in there with me. I didn't think nothin' was ever goin' to happen.

BRAD

Is that how you usually do it? Drag fly-boys into record booths with you?

(Mimics, mockingly)

"Have you heard this here new Doris Day record?"

EDGAR

I done that once before.

BRAD

Oh? Yeah? And what happened?

EDGAR

He let me do it to him right there, then he run away.

BRAD

Son of a bitch.

EDGAR

I seen him again on the street once with some of his friends, and he wouldn't even look at me.

BRAD

Son of a bitch.

EDGAR

I thought that's what you wanted.

BRAD (*Opening his sheet and wrapping* EDGAR *in it with him*).
You knew what I wanted.

EDGAR

I thought I did. I dreamed I did. When you finally touched the back of my pants—

BRAD

I thought my hand would burn.

EDGAR (*With a long, level look at* BRAD; *they are now kneeling face to face on the sofa, only their heads showing above the folds of the sheet*).
Touch me there.

BRAD

I can't. I'll kill you.

EDGAR

No, no. I'm all right. Touch it.

BRAD *(Chuckles)*.

With what?

EDGAR

Your hand. Like you did.

*(*BRAD *obviously does)*

Ah!

BRAD

Lena and her girlfriend are gonna be gone until Monday, right?

EDGAR *(Understanding)*.

Yes.

BRAD *(Begins a more elaborate manipulation under the sheet)*.

How do you know Lena?

EDGAR

She sold my folks their house. We kind of . . . you know . . . suspected about each other. From books? She was always askin' me to come over. I heard her and her girlfriend had parties over here with all guys. I was afraid. Ooooooo . . .

(This "Ooooooo . . ." is not from pain)

BRAD *(Never taking his eyes from* EDGAR'S, *despite what's happening under the sheet—a truly serious finger-fuck)*.

But you never came over?

EDGAR

Huh-uh. No. Oooo, yes.

BRAD

Good. Why?

EDGAR

I was scared. Why good?

BRAD

Because I couldn't stand it if you had. Why scared?

EDGAR

I was afraid the guys might be rough. Couldn't stand it why?

BRAD

If any other man had ever had you in a bed. Am I too rough?

EDGAR

I only done it with boys in a bed, when I was little. No, you're all right.

BRAD

But not like we do it, did you? Just all right?

EDGAR

Never like we do it. More scared.

BRAD

Scared of what? Answer my question.

EDGAR *(His mind on other things).*

What was I scared of?

BRAD

No, am I *just* all right?

EDGAR

God, you're everything. Can I come this way?

BRAD

Better not yet. Come into the bedroom.

EDGAR

I think I'm goin' to. I was scared I'd like them more than they liked me.

BRAD

Don't.

EDGAR

Come? Or like them?

BRAD *(Breathing pretty heavily himself)*.

Either. I don't want you seeing anybody else.

EDGAR

I don't want to see anybody else. Hell, I don't know anybody else. Do you think we can *make* it to the bedroom?

BRAD

I think you have to open your thighs first.

EDGAR

I don't think I can.

BRAD

Why? Are you cramped shut?

EDGAR

No, I just don't think I can bear to let go.

BRAD

Come on. I'll put somethin' else there.

*(*BRAD *disengages under the sheet)*

EDGAR *(After a little moan of disappointment)*.

Have you got a hard-on?

BRAD

I don't know if it's a hard-on or a charley horse. Either way, it'll do.

EDGAR

Can you come again?

BRAD

I don't care if I never come again. I just want to be in you.

EDGAR

Yes, yes, yes!

(They kiss passionately)

And then I want to be in you again.

BRAD *(Tugging* EDGAR *up from sofa; they are still wrapped in the sheet).*

Yeah, yeah, come on.

EDGAR

What if we can't get hard-ons?

BRAD

Then we'll do that other thing to each other.

EDGAR

Both at once? Can we? I bet we can! Sure we could!

BRAD

Sure, we can. And, yes, people do. Shut up and come on.

(Unwilling to let go of one another, they stumble hilariously toward bedroom, wrapped in sheet)

EDGAR

Can we do it to each other until we get hard-ons again?

BRAD

Baby, I get out of the Air Force in June. We can do it to each other for the rest of our lives. You see ...

(Stops, faces EDGAR*)*

... I'm scared of you, too.

EDGAR

You are?

BRAD

Yes. That's what I been tryin' to *tell* you.

EDGAR

We're scared of each other?

BRAD
I think so.

EDGAR
Really, truly, and deeply scared?

BRAD
I think so, yes. Ain't it the shits?

EDGAR
I was never scared of anybody before. Was you?

BRAD
Never.

EDGAR
I don't mean scared like when I was a kid.

BRAD
No.

EDGAR
I mean . . . responsibly and maturely scared.

BRAD
Yeah.

EDGAR
Scared in sickness and in health.

BRAD
For richer and for poorer.

EDGAR
Oh, God, do you mean that we're in . . . ?

BRAD
Go ahead, say it.

EDGAR
I can't.

BRAD

Say it or I'll laugh at you.

EDGAR

You'll laugh at me if I do say it.

BRAD

I can't laugh with my mouth full.

EDGAR

Your mouth's not full.

BRAD

Whose fault is that?

EDGAR

Are you and me ...?

BRAD

Say it.

EDGAR

Are we in ...?

BRAD

If you don't say it, I will.

EDGAR

No, I want to.

BRAD

We'll say it at the same time.

EDGAR

Whisper it.

BRAD

We can't reach each other's *ears* at the same time.

EDGAR

I bet we can if we try.

BRAD

There's no way.

EDGAR

Let's try. We're in—

BRAD

We're in—

EDGAR

We're in—

BRAD

We're—It can't be done.

EDGAR

We're in—*Love!*

BRAD

Go on, talk dirty, I love it.

EDGAR *(Suddenly taking the lead, dragging the resistant* BRAD *toward bedroom).*

Come on in here. I wanna do somethin' to you.

BRAD

What am I letting myself in for?

EDGAR

I want to do things to you *nobody* never done to you.

BRAD

How old are you, anyway, you hillbilly whore?

EDGAR

I'm nineteen, you New York nut.

BRAD

You're not a day over seventeen.

EDGAR

I'm seventeen. How old are you?

BRAD

I'm twenty-one.

EDGAR

Good, you're legal.

BRAD

Honey, none of us is legal.

EDGAR

I don't care. Come on into this bedroom with me. I'm goin' to think of somethin' nobody ever done to *nobody* before.

BRAD *(Happily)*.

Oh, God, I'm going to live in Drinking Water, New Mexico, for the rest of my *life*.

(EDGAR *drags him into the bedroom. The doorbell chimes. They pop out of the bedroom)*

BRAD

Oh, shit.

EDGAR

My folks.

BRAD

Vice cops.

EDGAR

Lena.

BRAD

Indians!

EDGAR

Pretend we're not here.

BRAD

They'll break in. They have tomahawks.

EDGAR

It's probably some friends of Lena's.

BRAD

Oh, shit, an orgy.

EDGAR

Orgy? Do people really—?

BRAD

Shut up, dimbo.

EDGAR

What'll we do?

BRAD

Answer it?

EDGAR

Get dressed?

BRAD

Shit, get dressed. Yes, God.

> *(They dress hurriedly, no time for socks or shoes. The mood is one of embarrassed, wanton hilarity rather than fear)*

EDGAR *(Of bottle).*

What if they think I been drinkin'? I'm not old enough to drink.

BRAD

Everybody drinks in these goddamned suburbs. You're not old enough to eat, that's the problem.

EDGAR

Don't worry. They can even torture me. I won't betray you.

BRAD

Just deny everything and keep a plug up your ass until I get out of the guardhouse.

EDGAR

Do all those guys do it in the guardhouse?

BRAD

I hope to hell I never get to know. Now shut your box, Pandora.

(They are sketchily dressed)

All right, baby. Remember I love you.

(He kisses EDGAR and pats the boy's rear)

And keep my place.

EDGAR

I liked the dirty way you said it better.

BRAD

Baby!

(Kisses EDGAR)

Shut up, okay? Let me handle this. Whoever.

(BRAD strikes a pose of manly capability and strides offstage to answer the front door. EDGAR gets into his jeans, T-shirt, and shirt and stands listening)

BRAD *(Offstage).*

Yes, can I help you?

CURTIS *(Offstage).*

Is this the residence of Miss Lena Schenck, Airman?

BRAD *(Offstage).*

Yes *sir!*

(At the sound of the SIR!, EDGAR stands still in fear)

CURTIS *(Offstage).*

May I see Miss Schenck?

BRAD *(Offstage).*

Miss Schenck isn't here, sir.

CURTIS *(Offstage).*

I see. When will she be here?

BRAD *(Offstage)*.

Monday morning, sir.

CURTIS *(Offstage)*.

What's your name, Airman?

BRAD *(Offstage)*.

Airman First Class Bradley Kowski, sir.

CURTIS *(Offstage)*.

And what are you doing here, Kowski?

BRAD *(Offstage)*.

I'm a friend of Miss Schenck's, sir.

CURTIS *(Offstage)*.

And you're staying here while she's away?

BRAD *(Offstage)*.

Yes sir. She's in Melrose visiting her mother, sir.

CURTIS *(Offstage)*.

Very well. Have you your pass, Airman?

BRAD *(Offstage)*.

Yes sir. Right here, sir.

CURTIS *(Offstage)*.

All right, Airman. Put it away.

BRAD *(Offstage)*.

Yessir.

CURTIS *(Offstage)*.

And stand at ease. We're not on base here.

BRAD *(Offstage)*.

Yes sir.

CURTIS *(Offstage, after a pause)*.

Very well. Will you tell Miss Schenck to call me Monday afternoon?

BRAD *(Offstage)*.
Yes sir.

CURTIS *(Offstage)*.
Do you want to take my telephone number?

BRAD *(Offstage)*.
Oh, yes sir. Sir.

CURTIS *(Offstage)*.
Do you have your notebook with you, Airman?

BRAD *(Offstage)*.
I'm afraid not, sir.

CURTIS *(Offstage)*.
Aren't you supposed always to have your notebook on your person, Airman?

BRAD *(Offstage)*.
Yessir. I am sir. I do sir. It's in there sir. I'll get it sir.

(BRAD re-enters, somewhat shaken. He shushes EDGAR and the two of them look frantically for notebook. Just as EDGAR locates it and hands it to BRAD , CAPTAIN GRAHAM CURTIS ambles in. He clicks on a bright white light, vanquishing the sunset mood. CURTIS is two or three years older than BRAD. He is a refined and educated person with clean good looks and fine posture. One cannot but wonder why he is only a captain)

CURTIS *(After a long, slow look at the whiskey, EDGAR, the sheet, the shoes lying about, and at BRAD)*.
Do you want to take that number now, Airman?

BRAD *(Holds notebook poised)*.
Yessir.

CURTIS
Captain Graham Curtis. 543-175.

BRAD *(Jotting furiously)*.
Yessir.

CURTIS *(Politely, to* EDGAR*).*

Hello, young man.

EDGAR

Yes *sir!*

CURTIS *(Amused).*

Are you in the Air Force, young man?

EDGAR

No *sir!*

CURTIS

Miss Schenck has ... all kinds of friends. That's all right. We're not after you men. ... Don't I know you, boy?

EDGAR

I don't think so, sir.

CURTIS

You don't have to call me "sir" if you're not in the Air Force, boy.

EDGAR

No sir.

CURTIS *(To* BRAD*).*

I saw only one car in Miss Schenck's driveway. How did you get here?

BRAD

Ed—the young man drove me, sir.

CURTIS

I see.

(To EDGAR*)*

Don't you work at La Cima? Aren't you ... a busboy or whatever they call it?

EDGAR

Yes sir.

CURTIS

I thought so. You work at the Officers' Luncheon on Mondays.

EDGAR

Yes sir. Oh, yes sir. I seen you, sir.

CURTIS

Damned good restaurant for out here.

(To BRAD*)*

Look, we're trying to avoid trouble. Some busybody reported to the Air Police that Miss Schenck is receiving large numbers of men here. They think Miss Schenck and her . . . friend . . . are . . . running a . . . house of ill fame.

(To EDGAR, *smiling)*

Do you know what that is, boy?

EDGAR *(Much relieved).*

Yes sir. A whorehouse. With girls.

CURTIS

That's right. That's what they think.

*(*CURTIS *saunters around the room, then wanders off into the bedroom)*

EDGAR *(Whispers).*

Wow! He thinks it's just a whorehouse!

BRAD

SShhhhh!

CURTIS *(Re-enters).*

Well, that's all, gentlemen. Tell the woman to call me. All we want is for her to stop what she's doing. We don't want a scandal. We don't want to report her to the local police. Do you understand that?

BRAD

Oh, yes, sir.

CURTIS

Is the other woman gone too, this . . . Miss Franklin?

BRAD

Yes sir.

CURTIS

I see . . . Tell them what I told you. And cheer up, Airman. Nobody wants any trouble. The Air Force understands that you fellows have to have . . . some such facility. Understand?

BRAD *(Man-to-man).*

Oh, yes sir, I understand, sir.

CURTIS *(To* EDGAR*).*

Boy, don't you think that you ought to go home?

EDGAR

Yes sir.

(He heads for door)

CURTIS

Don't you think you ought to put on your shoes first?

EDGAR

Oh. Yes sir.

*(*EDGAR *walks to the pile of his and* BRAD*'s shoes, which happens to be directly in front of* CURTIS*. Unable to take his eyes off* CURTIS*'s,* EDGAR *bends and comes up with one of his shoes and one of* BRAD*'s. He kneels again before* CURTIS *and comes up with his own shoes, and has to kneel again for his socks.)*

CURTIS *(Grinning amiably).*

Okay. Now go into the bathroom and put them on. And comb your hair.

*(*EDGAR *starts off)*

Wait. Let me smell your breath.

EDGAR

Yes, sir!

(He walks back to CURTIS, *stands on tiptoe, and breathes into* CURTIS'*s face)*

I don't drink none, sir.

CURTIS

Good boy. Now go comb that hair and get decent, and you can take the Airman away.

EDGAR

Yes *sir!*

*(*EDGAR *runs off happily to bathroom, with a smile at* BRAD*)*

BRAD *(Easy and relaxed).*

Thank you for the warning, sir. I'll certainly tell Miss Schenck and Miss Franklin everything you—

CURTIS *(Cold, angry).*

Christ, how old is that boy?

BRAD

I . . . don't know, sir.

CURTIS

Well, get his ass home and get back to the base.

BRAD *(At attention).*

Yes sir.

CURTIS

Are you taking money from him?

BRAD

What? No sir.

CURTIS

Kowski, is it?

BRAD

Yes sir. Bradley Kowski.

CURTIS

From. . . ?

BRAD

New York, sir. The Bronx, sir.

CURTIS

New York. The Bronx. I see. Airman?

BRAD

Yes sir?

CURTIS

Let me smell your hands.

BRAD

Sir?

CURTIS

Your hands, Kowski.

(BRAD *is halfway across the room from* CURTIS. *Shamefacedly, he raises his hands and takes a step toward* CURTIS. CURTIS *stops him with a gesture.*)

CURTIS

That's enough. Look, Airman, it's obvious what's going on. I'm going to talk turkey. How long do you have to serve?

BRAD

Three months, five days, sir.

CURTIS

Don't you think you should forego the pleasure of seeing this child for at least three months and six days, Kowski?

BRAD

I don't know what you mean, sir.

CURTIS

Oh, shall I make it plainer? Fine. One of the queens that comes here got nervous and came to me. She's afraid there'll be an investigation and fortunately I was on duty when she came in. Do you get me?

BRAD

No sir.

CURTIS

Well, you had better get me. I'm not Air Police, Airman, I am O.S.I., and ferreting out fairies is one of our jobs. You tell those dykes to latch onto a couple of straight locals and have them over here. And you and your boyfriends keep yourselves *real* clean for a while. If Miss Schenck wants to be a queen bee, you tell her to stick to the town faggots and leave the Air Force out of it. The office is investigating a fag cook at the local hotel that's been fondling fly-boys' flies in the men's room, and there is nothing my chief would like better than a nice roundup of nancies to give him a good mark. Do I make myself clear?

EDGAR *(Re-enters, repaired).*

I guess I'll go now, sir. Are you ready, Mister Kowski?

CURTIS

Do I make myself clear, Airman Kowski?

BRAD

Yes sir. Clear, sir.

CURTIS *(To* EDGAR*).*

I think it would be better if you didn't come around here again, boy. . . . What's your name?

EDGAR

Uh . . . Edgar, sir.

(He senses a changed atmosphere)

CURTIS

Edgar what?

EDGAR

Edgar Brown, sir.

(He tries to look at BRAD, *who stands sternly at attention.)*

CURTIS

Come here, EDGAR. Don't be afraid.

(Maneuvers EDGAR *to where* EDGAR *and* BRAD *cannot see one another's faces)*

They call you Eddie?

EDGAR

Usually Edgar, sir.

CURTIS *(with sincere care)*

Okay, Edgar. Now, nothing's going to happen to you—or to Miss Schenck—if I can help it. But that means you'll have to cooperate, do you hear me?

EDGAR

Yes, sir.

CURTIS

Don't be upset. Everything is going to be all right. Do you trust me?

EDGAR

Yes, sir.

CURTIS

Then listen to me very closely. Nothing is going to be done to you. Nothing you've done is wrong. You just have to be very careful, or big bad men like me will have to do what they have to do. You wouldn't want Miss Schenck or Miss Franklin to get into trouble, would you?

EDGAR

Oh, no sir.

CURTIS

You wouldn't want any of the airmen who come here to get into trouble, either, would you?

EDGAR

No, no sir.

CURTIS

And you wouldn't want Airman Kowski thrown in the guardhouse and then kicked out of the service, would you?

EDGAR

Oh, no, sir.

CURTIS

Then look at me. How old are you?

EDGAR

Eighteen, sir.

CURTIS

When?

EDGAR

... In eight months, sir.

CURTIS

Now, don't be nervous. Will you promise me you won't see Airman Kowski for eight months, then?

EDGAR (*Looks at* BRAD, *who gives a quick nod*).
Yes, sir.

CURTIS

Look at *me*! You just keep your nose clean and play with whatever little friends your own age you have, you hear me?

EDGAR

Yes, sir ...

CURTIS *(Ruffles* EDGAR's *hair).*

You're a fine boy. Now go along and get straight home. Do your parents know where you are?

EDGAR

Oh, no, sir. They're out of town all weekend.

CURTIS

Then you shouldn't have any trouble, should you, now?

EDGAR

No, sir.

BRAD

We'll go now, Edgar.

(Heads for his shoes)

EDGAR

Sure.

CURTIS

As you were, Kowski.

*(*BRAD *freezes)*

You go ahead, Edgar.

EDGAR *(To* BRAD*).*

Is it all right?

CURTIS

It's all right. Go home, Edgar. I'll drop you at a bus stop, Airman.

EDGAR

But—

BRAD

But—

CURTIS

Cool it, Kowski. You may go, Edgar. . . . I'll see you at La Cima this Monday, won't I?

EDGAR
Yes, sir.

CURTIS
All right. You ... don't have to show that you know me. Understand?

EDGAR
Yes, sir.

CURTIS *(after a pause, feigned casualness)*
Is Edgar your father's name, too?

EDGAR
Huh? Yes, sir. Are you goin' to tell my father anything, sir?

CURTIS
Of course not. You go home and be sure you stay right there the rest of this weekend, you hear me?

EDGAR
Yes, sir. Goodbye, sir. Goodbye, Airman Kowski.
*(*EDGAR *starts out)*

BRAD
Edgar—with your permission sir—Edgar, aren't you going to take your records?

EDGAR *(Goes to phonograph, takes only one).*
I'll take my "Chances Are." ... I don't want "Secret Love."
(At door, to CURTIS*)*
I'll be seeing you on Monday, sir.
*(*EDGAR *exits)*

BRAD *(Still at attention).*
... Sir?

CURTIS
Relax, Kowski. At ease. Sit down.
(Giggles, kicks BRAD*'s shoes)*

Put on your shoes.

    (Sighs)

Can I possibly have a drink?

    BRAD *(Sits, springs up)*.

Oh, yes, sir.

    CURTIS

I'll get it. Sit down.

    *(*BRAD *does)*

This glass will do.

    (Pours drink)

Are you all right?

    (Drinks thirstily)

    BRAD *(Puzzled, donning socks and shoes)*.

Yes sir.

    CURTIS

Well, if anything happens, it's better it doesn't happen to a clean kid, isn't it?

    (We hear EDGAR*'s car starting up and pulling away)*

    BRAD

Yes sir.

    CURTIS

Oh, drop the sir. Call me Mary.

    *(*BRAD *blinks)*

Shit, I hope I did the right thing. You've got me over a barrel, I guess you know that.

    BRAD

I have, sir?

    CURTIS

If the investigation is carried through, all you have to do to get my ass sacked is tell them I didn't report this.

BRAD

Oh. Yeah. I guess so. Sir.

CURTIS

Of course, you wouldn't do that because it would get you in a sling, too.

BRAD

No, sir. Yes, sir.

CURTIS

But don't think that if you get caught, that ratting on me will make it any easier on you.

BRAD

No, sir.

CURTIS

If either one of us gets in a jam, remember that little boy will be up to his neck in it too, don't forget.

BRAD

Sir—

CURTIS

God, I hope he realizes that. White people aren't Catholic out here, are they? He won't feel moved to confess? The whole thing's *very* confusing.

BRAD

Yes, sir.

CURTIS

I'm trying to stop it. Or limit it to the damned fools that make trouble for everybody. Jesus, seventeen! What were you trying to do?

BRAD

I didn't know he was seventeen.

CURTIS

What did you think he was, retarded? What's the matter, you don't go for the other queens who hang out here?

BRAD

I hadn't been here before. Neither had . . .

CURTIS

Edgar.

BRAD

Edgar.

CURTIS

Silly name to hang on such a good-looking boy. So how did you wind up here?

BRAD

Edgar . . . the kid knew about it, sir.

CURTIS

. . . My name's Graham.

(Extends hand. They shake)

BRAD

. . . Brad.

CURTIS *(Still holding* BRAD*'s hand).*

Brad.

(Drops hand)

So! Brad! You still haven't answered my question. You don't look dumb. What were you doing with that kid?

BRAD

Well, I—

GRAHAM *(Embarrassed little laugh).*

I don't mean that literally, of course. Anyone could see—or imagine—I mean, what are you doing with a boy that *age?*

*(*BRAD *shrugs)*

You know what you could do *to* him, don't you? Get him beat to shit by his father. Make hell of his life at school. Get him locked up for life in a looney bin if his folks have influence enough.

BRAD

I won't see him again.

CURTIS

Jesus, just . . . you know . . . be careful. Wait until he's at least of age, hard as that might be. Or stick to the sluts in the barracks. You ought to be able to get all of them you want. . . . That was a compliment.

BRAD

Oh, thanks.

CURTIS

Just . . . watch yourself. A man has to develop a sense of discretion. Take me. When I saw what it was going to be like out here, I rented myself a little place in town, across the tracks, unlikely to be observed. Nothing fancy, but it's isolated. I felt it would be a safe place to . . . take men.

BRAD

I see.

CURTIS *(Pouring another drink)*.

Not that I've used it. Except to drink in. I haven't found many interesting people here. None, really. None that I'd care to risk exposure for. Or be alone in an isolated house with.

BRAD *(Realizing their isolation)*.

Yeah.

CURTIS

Oh, forgive me. Have a drink.

*(*BRAD *hesitates)*

Go ahead.

(Smiles)

I'm driving.

BRAD

Yeah. Well. Sure. Okay.

(Pours himself a drink)

CURTIS

So . . . How long have you been out here, Kowski? Brad?

BRAD

Eighteen months.

CURTIS

This your first time West?

BRAD

Yeah.

CURTIS

My first in New Mexico. We used to winter in California, of course. I'm from Pennsylvania, but I went to Yale. I used to get to New York a lot, actually. I'm surprised I don't remember you from there.

BRAD

You probably mean Manhattan. I never went there much.

CURTIS

No? I would have thought that would have been the safest place.

BRAD

For what?

CURTIS

For sex.

BRAD

Oh. You mean those bars. No. No, I didn't like those places.

CURTIS

I never did either, really. Afraid I'd see someone who knew me. So! What did you do? For sex?

BRAD

There was somebody, whenever I wanted it. I didn't do much.

CURTIS

Funny. I always thought of you . . . Bronx types cutting through hundreds of men. So! Have you been pretty active here?

BRAD

No. I can't stand quick blow-jobs in the barracks. Or drunk businessmen in parked cars out on the desert.

CURTIS

They call it "prairie."

(The two Easterners laugh. CURTIS *pours another drink)*

I've been pretty . . . circumspect myself.

(Laughs)

God, this is starting to sound like a dormitory seduction scene, isn't it?

(Pours BRAD *a drink)*

BRAD

I wouldn't know.

CURTIS

I'm sorry. That was a comment, not a hint. Besides . . . that kid must just about have burned you out. . . . How long had you two been here?

BRAD

Since Friday night. . . . I'm all right.

CURTIS

Do you . . . want to talk about it?

BRAD

What are you after? Dirty stories?

CURTIS

No. I make up the dirty stories myself. I always thought of myself as pretty refined, sensitive, you know? Then I found myself stuck out here with those ... pigs! ... in the barracks, and all the cowboys and rancheros on the town streets in those ... tight jeans ... and I found out how coarse I really am. No, I take care of the dirty stories myself. This isn't a dirty story, is it?

BRAD

Me and Edgar? No. No. We're in ... He's a nice kid. Very nice kid. Look, he won't get into any trouble, will he?

CURTIS

Not if you both cooperate.

(BRAD *bridles*)

Oh, stop it. I didn't mean—

BRAD

Mean what? Didn't mean what?

CURTIS

What you're obviously thinking. Or what I'm obviously thinking and trying to pretend I'm not. Look, just to clear the air: you're attractive as hell and I'm lonely as hell. But I'm not trying to pressure you into anything. God! If you want a quick, easy, sexual release, try me. Or if I'm for some reason or another not your type, I can put you in touch with a couple of officers that can treat you real nice. Hell, you might get one of them off of my ass. I don't mean that literally; I wouldn't put out for rank. God! I never heard myself talk like this before. And you, poor thing, having to sit there and listen to this ... adolescent self-discovery. Lord, I used to fantasize situations like this at Yale.

BRAD

Situations like what?

CURTIS

Having some strapping soldier at my command, under my thumb, and giving him sexual orders.

(BRAD *stands, shocked and angry*)

Oh, sit down.

(BRAD *does*)

That's what I'm *not* doing. God, it would be so easy, though. Do you realize what a fraught situation this is? Do you know what I mean?

BRAD

Yeah. Fraught. I read English.

CURTIS

I *have* you under my thumb. You have me. We both have Edgar. He has both of us. But he wouldn't do anything like that, would he? I mean, threaten, blackmail us. He seems like such a sweet kid. Tell me about Edgar. Edgar and you. If you want to. Is he? A sweet kid?

BRAD

He's very nice. He's . . . clean. I don't know what he is. Why are you asking?

CURTIS

God, I envy you. I saw the look on your face. You were actually more worried about that kid than about yourself. That's beautiful.

BRAD

Curtis—

CURTIS

Graham, please. I've been so damned lonely.

BRAD

Are you trying to get me to fix you up with Edgar?

CURTIS

Brad! No! The thought never entered my . . . sure, yes, I'd love it, who wouldn't? But I'd never actually do—! When I came in here, I wanted to get down on the floor with both of you. This room reeks of sex, can't you smell it? What do you think I am? I'm a man. I smell come, I'm excited. You really ought to bathe before you go back. You don't smell like a woman.

BRAD

Anybody that would know that isn't going to say anything.

CURTIS *(Pouring another drink).*

Hah! They're the ones most likely to say something. I learned that a long time ago at Yale. God, you look like something I'd make up in the dark before masturbating. All right, this is enough of this.

(Downs drink, clinks glass down)

Let's go.

BRAD *(Stands).*

Okay. If that's the way it is.

(Starts to peel off shirt)

CURTIS

No! Hey, no, I didn't mean that! I mean, let's get out. I'll drop you at a bus stop.

BRAD

Curtis, what is it you want? You've got me all mixed up.

CURTIS *(integrity fighting against lust)*

I want to get out of here and save us all some trouble. I want you and that kid to get together when the time comes. I want to save the kind ladies who run this whorehouse. I want some peace.

BRAD *(tempting, teasing)*

You sure you don't want to get your rocks off first?

CURTIS

Listen, take the red light out of your window. I'm having a hard enough time just keeping my hands off of you.

BRAD

You interrupted us at a pretty hot time, that's all. I'm sorry I misunderstood you.

CURTIS

I'm . . . you didn't misunderstand me. I keep thinking of Edgar.

BRAD

Oh, yes?

CURTIS

You and him, I mean. I just wish we could have met under ...
different circumstances.

BRAD

You and Edgar.

CURTIS

No! You and I.

BRAD

Maybe we will.

CURTIS

I'd ... like that. Thank you. For not judging me at my worst. Poor
Edgar.

BRAD

Why poor Edgar?

CURTIS

Getting left out.

BRAD

Oh.

CURTIS

Will he be all right?

BRAD

You mean if we go to bed?

CURTIS

No, I mean ... is he going to be shaken by all this?

BRAD

Shit, sure, what do you think? I don't know. I just met him.

CURTIS

But he's more than just a trick.

BRAD

I don't know. What are you trying to get me to say? I'm a lonely soldier. I picked him up at a record store. I thought he was the only nice queer in town.

CURTIS

He probably thought the same thing about you. Christ, this'll probably ruin him. If only there was some way he could have an affair with a nice, caring, loving man . . .

BRAD

I was going to call him.

CURTIS

I thought you were.

BRAD

I figured *you* were.

CURTIS

Why?

BRAD

"Is Edgar your father's name, too?"

CURTIS

Oh.

BRAD

Were you?

(Undoes his belt, slowly)

CURTIS

I admit I thought of checking up on him.

BRAD

That's a nice thought.

CURTIS

I hope it was.

BRAD

Was it?

CURTIS

God, I don't know.

BRAD

Mister, I think you need to let off some steam.
(Undoes his pants)

CURTIS

I think I'm about to, just standing here. Do you have to expose yourself that way?

BRAD

I don't know any way to get my shirt tail tucked in regulation without unbuttoning my pants first.

CURTIS

You'd think I'd be used to men in uniform by now.

BRAD

You need some sex to clear your head of all these fantasies.
(BRAD puts his cap on at a rakish angle)

CURTIS

My worst fantasy is getting caught doing this.

BRAD *(Moves slowly toward CURTIS)*.

How important is it, really, that we get out of here?

CURTIS

It could be . . . very important.

BRAD

Why? Are the Air Police coming?

CURTIS

No. I'm about to.

BRAD

Do you wanna ... lie down for a while?

CURTIS

I just wouldn't want you to think I'm insisting on it.

BRAD

Listen, the more you get, the more you want. I'd like to see what you're made of.

CURTIS

It wouldn't take me long.

BRAD

I could do you a few times. It'll take me a while to get warmed up, anyway. You were right. That hot kid did wear me out. Don't I still smell like him?

(He is very near CURTIS *by now)*

CURTIS *(About to take the one step between them).*

Is all of this ... just to protect Edgar?

BRAD *(Turns and walks away).*

Christ, I wouldn't have your mind for a million dollars.

CURTIS

I'm sorry, it was just a thought.

BRAD *(Corrects his clothes).*

Look, if he's on your mind, call him.

CURTIS

That would be the worst kind of hypocrisy.

BRAD

I meant to reassure him, not to fuck him.

CURTIS

Oh.

BRAD

Graham, you have a dirty mind.

CURTIS

I'm a little confused right now, that's all.
(Picks up drink)

BRAD

So . . . do you want to try me now, and see that child on Monday, or what do you want to do?

CURTIS *(Sits on sofa, finishes his drink, then—).*
Can we still do it?

BRAD

Sure. I'm startin' to pop my pants right here.

CURTIS

I thought you said you were burned out.

BRAD

What you've got me thinkin' has brought it back to life.

CURTIS

Would it be better to do it here or go to my place?

BRAD

You got a phone at your place?

CURTIS

Sure. You've got the number.

BRAD

That's the number you gave me for Miss Schenck to call?

CURTIS

That's right. I didn't want her calling the office about *this*.

BRAD

But you said for her to call you Monday afternoon.

CURTIS

That's right.

BRAD

You don't have to be in your office Monday?

CURTIS

No. Things are quiet now. I usually stay in town Monday. Makes it easier to get to the ... Officer's Luncheon.

BRAD

So. It's Saturday evening now. That means we can have tonight, and Sunday, and all of Monday, too.

CURTIS

How long is your pass for?

BRAD

Sunday night. You could fix it.

CURTIS (*his last play for power*)

Yes. I could. If you're good enough.

BRAD (*accepting the challenge*)

Okay ... Let's go?

CURTIS

Okay.

(*Rises and crosses almost to door. Stops*)

You're ... not just trying to fuck me out so I don't go to Edgar, are you?

BRAD

What do you care?

CURTIS

I do care ... very much.

BRAD

Let's see how we feel on Monday.

CURTIS
We who?

BRAD
We whoever.
(Very close to CURTIS*)*
I'm goin' to go crazy if we don't leave.

CURTIS
I think I have. I have some decent whiskey at my place.

BRAD
We won't need it. You're decent whiskey.

CURTIS
It's nice to have it anyway.
(Straightens cap, turns out light. Sunset blazes)
When we drive through town, keep your head down.

BRAD
Oh, it'll be down, old buddy. You're gonna have to work hard to keep your mind on your drivin'.
(They exchange a long look. CURTIS *exits.* BRAD *slips "Secret Love" record inside his shirt and exits.)*

BRAD *(Offstage).*
Hey! Some car, Captain Curtis!

C U R T A I N

1960s

FOG

for Bill Haislip

FOG

The setting is a clearing in Central Park, a section called The Ramble, where, late at night, when the law says the Park must be cleared, the city's homosexuals meet and mate, for it is the sixties.

The time is early autumn, near midnight, when a freak fog has blanketed the Park in a darkness not even penetrable by the streetlights, which have, anyway, been broken by men who don't want a bright light on their doings.

We hear foghorns off right. A STUD enters. He is in his twenties, well-built, tall, very handsome, well-groomed, wearing a puce raglan sweater and Nile green hip-huggers. He is walking very carefully, orienting himself by pausing to listen for the occasional bursts of the foghorn. He does this with a visible sense of humor, tilting his ear until the blast sounds, then taking a few more steps with a follow-me gesture as if leading troops.

After the STUD is a few steps onstage, and waiting, a FAG enters from the opposite side. He is small, thin, nellie, in Jackie Kennedy sunglasses, a Beatles wig, pointy boots, and a chic Cardin suit. He gropes uncertainly before himself, feeling tentatively with an almost balletic toe the familiar turf.

They approach each other silently, utterly unable to see. Since FAG's hands are out before him right at the level of STUD's crotch, an embarrassing encounter is just about to take place.

But a new foghorn sounds from off left, and STUD *speaks just before* FAG'*s hands would hit his Nile green crotch.*

STUD

Hey! I know I'm not walkin' in that small a circle!

(Off left foghorn sounds again)

No fair movin' the fuckin' foghorns!

(Off right horn sounds again, then the left one sounds)

Two foghorns. I stand disgusted. In a freak fog. Somewhere in Central Park.

FAG *(Cautiously).*

Yes, there's two of them.

STUD *(Mock frightened).*

Who dere?

FAG *(Though his high voice would not encourage fears).*

Don't worry. I'm not a mugger or a rapist or anything.

STUD

Aw, come on. You must be something. Or maybe not. Anyway, you couldn't find me in this benighted fog, anyway. Befogged night.

FAG *(After pause).*

Are you?

STUD

What? Befogged? Or benighted?

FAG *(Impatient with jokes).*

A rapist. Or mugger.

STUD

Relax, you're safe. I couldn't find you, either. We're probably the safest two people who ever met at night in Central Park.

(Unable to resist teasing)

Unless one of us is a cop.

FAG

Oh, damn; are you?

STUD

I wouldn't tell you if I was, would I? But relax. I'm not a cop. I'm not a mugger. I'm a . . . vailable. The only people in Central Park at this time of night are either cops or available.

FAG

It often amounts to the same thing.

STUD

I'm not even available at the moment. I just used that as a technical term.

FAG

Well! You're perfectly safe. I wouldn't try to force myself on anyone. To be just brutally frank, I was out here following a tall, silent number in a puce raglan pullover from a party.

STUD

Well, relax. I just came from quite another party and I'm in a maroon crew-neck. What's puce, exactly?

FAG

A color.

STUD

And what's raglan?

FAG

How long have you *been* in New York?

STUD

Too long.

FAG

I mean, one usually picks up things like puce and raglan.

STUD *(Laughs).*

Well, I hope you pick it up. How is the action in the Park on a night like this?

FAG

Well, I never tried before on a night like this. But I saw him walk into the Park and I said what the hell; faint heart ne'er won fair laddy. Then the fog fell and I lost him.

STUD

You're lost, too, huh? Hell.

FAG

Me? I know this park like a book. He's lost, though.

STUD

I've never been here before. At night, I mean. Like this. Maybe you could show me the way out?

FAG

Actually I thought I'd browse around for a bit.

STUD

Expecting to luck across him?

FAG

Or somebody. When the fog lifts.

STUD *(Struck by the words)*.

When the fog lifts.

(It's amazing how mournful a couple of distant foghorns can sound when you're in a melancholy mood)

Tell me something: what does it matter to you about the fog lifting?

FAG *(Filing his nails)*.

I don't understand.

STUD

I mean . . . why aren't you looking for somebody now?

FAG

Wellll . . . I sort of am.

STUD

No, no, I mean . . . you want to wait till the fog lifts so you can see what they look like, right?

FAG

Sure.

STUD

Let me tell you something. . . . What do you do?

FAG

Well, I'm game for just about anything.

STUD *(Laughs)*.

No, that's not what I meant. I meant, for a living. What is your work? What is your life?

FAG

Oh, *that*. I'm a window decorator.

STUD

And are you good at it?

FAG

Well, not to brag, but I've been told I'm one of the most sought-after window decorators in the greater New York–New Jersey area. I work where I want, when I want, and I've even designed scenery for a couple of plays. Off-Off Broadway.

STUD

I think that's wonderful.

FAG

Well, thank you. Most people laugh.

STUD

How can you let them?

FAG

Well, you know. Window decorators, hairdressers . . . most people laugh.

STUD

Yeah? Now wait. This puce raglan number—this strong, silent type—what does he do?

FAG

Anything he wants to, baby, believe me.

STUD

Seriously, please.

FAG

I don't know, I just saw him tonight.

STUD

Did you even talk to him?

FAG

No, as I said, he was pretty strong and silent.

STUD

But you're trailing him out here in the cold and wet and dark, risking mugging and raping and arrest and God knows what kind of humiliation and—my God, infection—just on the off chance that maybe—I repeat, maybe—you can mouse around with him in the bushes for a little while. My God, it sounds like a duel. And you don't even get a choice of weapons; that's up to him.

FAG

Well, that's how it is.

STUD

But good lord, man, here you are, capable and respected and talented, and you're letting a probable lout like that shove you around. Why? Can you tell me why?

FAG

Well, he was *very* good looking. He looked like a weight lifter, maybe. He was collegiate, which I like, and he had on these Nile green pants without pockets—they're called hip-huggers, dear—and he was showing just fantastic basket . . .

(The foghorns sound. STUD *realizes it is he who is being described)*

STUD

Jesus. Nile green, huh?

FAG

Oh, Mary, yes!

STUD

Well, do you have any idea why this puce— What does that *mean,* by the way?

FAG

It's a sort of earthy red-brown shade.

STUD

Not much like maroon, huh?

FAG

Oh, no; maroon is more of a chocolaty-purple.

STUD

And raglan?

FAG

That means the sleeve seams are set above the shoulder.

STUD *(There is no doubt that he is the prey).*

I'll bet not many people know that.

FAG

Really? Well, it's nothing to know.

STUD *(Feeling his raglan seams).*

Jesus. Well, tell me, anyway: why do you think this guy left the party?

FAG

Obviously because there was no one there as attractive as he.

STUD

As he. Okay. Let me put it this way: Why do you think he was so silent?

FAG

Because that works best.

STUD

Let me tell you—I haven't been in New York long enough to get smart, mind you—but let me tell you why I think he was so fucking . . . strong and silent.

FAG

I don't usually like generalizations.

STUD

You listen to me or I'll call a cop. Or a mugger. Let me guess about that party. I'll bet that only half the people there knew each other.

FAG

Well, that's always best.

STUD

Sure, because nobody wants anybody that they know. Or maybe it's anybody that knows them. But, whichever, I'll bet half the guys there—and on an early Autumn, high-season night like this there were only guys there—

FAG

You're wrong—

STUD *(Quickly)*.

Unless maybe the host's Southern . . . aunt.

FAG

His sister. His Southern sister was there. That's very clever of you.

STUD

These parties are all alike. I just came from . . . practically . . . the same party myself. Let me go on. Half of the guys there were like yourself: young to not-so-young businessmen, artists, writers, lawyers, whatever the group happens to center around—

FAG

Yes! Yes!

STUD

And the other half—the half nobody knew—they were equally—half-and-half of the half—divided between little giddy make-up queens that are invited to make everybody else look good by comparison (besides which, give 'em enough to drink or smoke and they're a sure, if somewhat undesirable, thing) and a number of strong, silent types in easy-off puce cozies and Nile green basket-wrappers, invited from a number of bars and drugstores and ... elevators where they were available because they don't have much to do besides window-decorate themselves in pubic puce and gimme-green and wait around for an invitation to a party ... of two or three or thirty. Any number can play!

FAG

How long did you say you'd been in New York?

STUD *(After a foghorn sounds)*.

Can I tell you a little about myself?

FAG

Because, really, that was funny the way you described that party. It's just exactly the one that I was at, but I couldn't describe it nearly as well. You should be a writer.

STUD *(Quietly)*.

Thank you. I sort of halfway wanted to be one ... but I found out my looks were against me.

FAG

Oh, really?

STUD

I'm not very attractive.

(Long pause)

I guess you won't want to talk to me anymore.

FAG

Well, there's nothing else to do till the fog ... Uh, you say your looks were against you becoming a writer? What have looks got to do with that?

STUD

Well, you see, when I was seventeen—

FAG

How old are you now?

STUD *(Who is in his mid-twenties).*

I'm ... eighteen.

FAG

Oh, well, maybe there's something you can do about your looks. Yeast tablets and things.

STUD

That's what all my friends say to me. You see, I was very scrawny at seventeen, and pimply. But still I had hope, y'know?

FAG *(Sighs, unheard).*

I know.

STUD

I thought if I came to New York, people wouldn't mind all that. . . . That here, in the center of the world's talent and achievement, they'd only care if a person had talent, was talented, that they'd care for a person for their—I don't know—his character, his *self* ...

(Stops, fighting tears)

FAG

... Are you still there?

STUD

Yeah. Yeah. I'm here. I thought maybe you had gone away. I mean, I know my voice is pretty resonant and I thought maybe

you had only been staying because you thought I was good looking.

(FAG *shrugs but does not answer*)

Well, anyway. I got here. And started meeting people. And it was
just as I'd pictured.

(*He acts out the scenes he describes, moving about, pantomiming, so
that* Fag *is constantly getting his voice from different directions*)

They didn't mind that I was gawky and skinny and hunched and
pimply. They found out I was a writer and started inviting me to
their parties. I wore a funny suit and I st-st-stuttered, and I noticed
that nobody was taking me home, but I thought, "Well, it's just a
matter of time; concerned with talent and character as they are,
they have to get to know a person; they're not like the men who
grab you in the subways." And then I noticed that while these
aristocrats were getting to know me, while they were saying their
warm and sincere goodbyes to me at their doors, there were always
a couple of people still inside. Friends, I thought. But after being
at a couple of parties at any one person's house, I noticed that
those were always different friends who stayed on as the door
closed in my face. I noticed sweaters and tight pants like a uniform.
Or like the costumes of some endless chorus line.

(*He mimics the poses of half-a-dozen butch numbers*)

Pow! Zam! Blat! Baloo! Whiz! Bang! And so I began to get nervous. Then I began to notice while at these parties, these parties
given by and for the artists, the lawyers, the businessmen, the mak-
ers and rulers of the sacred mind of man, I seldom heard those
professions deeply propounded. Seldom? Nay, never. It worked very
curiously. Upon discovering that the leaning tower of bones and
pimples was a young writer, professors of literature, themselves
legends from looming universities, would slide to my side for the
opportunity to describe in learned prose some wedge-shaped un-
employable sitting strong and silent in a corner. And I, who stood
there with my thumb in a martini, listening to these learned and
powerful men, and yearning after their intelligence, their approval,
their acumen and admiration, I . . . I would slowly realize that the
gist of their panegyrics was that I, I, being younger and therefore

theoretically standing more of a chance than they, should stumble over and sample a hunk of the hunk.

(Waits for response. None is forthcoming. He screams.)
Do you know what I mean?

FAG *(Startled).*

Well, that's life. Everyone wants the beauties.

STUD

I *don't!* . . . I mean, I don't care. It's not what I'm after.

FAG

Well, I mean, that's life.

STUD

That's what?

FAG *(Screams back).*

That's life!

STUD *(Trying to regain composure and reason).*

Look, do you remember how I started on all this raving?

FAG

It's very interesting. I know what you mean. Everybody's after the beauties, and they're after each other, or else they drive a person broke or drunk or crazy, but that's—

STUD *(Screams).*

Don't say that again!

(Silence. Foghorns. More reasonably.)

Please. Listen. Remember I started out to tell you what I thought was the reason for these characters, these puce and Nile products, being so strong and silent?

FAG

Oh. That. Yes.

STUD

They're specialists themselves. They don't have any small talk. They have to spend so much time lifting weights and directing their barbers and studying various poses in mirrors that they have no time to think of anything else, no ... time ... to develop any abilities they might have. They sit around, in awe of the talents in the room with them. They want those people's love, and they're scared to death to open their mouths. Until they find out that these people only became specialists in law or art or ... literature ... because they didn't think they could make it as specialists in beauty.

FAG

Well, I'm not sure I see just what it is you're driving at.

STUD

Remember, I'm seventeen. I'm skinny and scrawny.

FAG

Well, you sure don't sound it.

STUD

I've developed my voice by talking with my mouth full of hors d'oeuvres. But I'm seventeen, and scrawny and pimply—

FAG

I thought you said you were eighteen.

STUD

That was a lie. I'm still ... still seventeen.

FAG (*In the tone of a pep talk*).

Well, then, don't despair so. As I said before, we live in a marvelous age for somebody young enough, and if you'll just apply yourself, you can certainly do *something* about your—

STUD

Oh, I will, I will. In the next eight years I'll lift weights and improve my posture and eat sea salt and get good haircuts and stop talking at parties and get my full glandular growth and pick up my chorus outfits in the men's-men's stores and develop a strong, silent countenance to cover the fact that I haven't read any good books lately, and everyone will stop talking to me at parties and start taking *about* me and I'll get to be a star attraction on the smarty-arty-party circuit and I'll get disgusted and stop even dreaming

about writing because it'll seem to me that there's no one to write
for.

STUD FAG

Well, then, I fail to see the problem. If you can do all that, and get
the people you want—

STUD

But, oh, God, I never will get them. They'll lie there on the Persian
carpet making it with each other after hustling the host's sister
away, looking through the gold Florentine candelabra on the floor
at the part of me corresponding to whatever part of each other, or
themselves, they're working on, because they're too afraid of me
to—

FAG

Oh, come now, surely not everybody—

STUD

But it's just as bad if they do get the courage to come over the
candelabra, because if they do . . . Did you ever take L.S.D.?

FAG *(Automatically holds out his hand to receive some)*.
No.

STUD

Well, please don't think I'm one of those sick queens who takes
anything anybody offers them—
(FAG *withdraws hand)*
—but once I had L.S.D.

FAG *(Making a sudden connection)*.
Wait, did you say Florentine candleabra?

STUD

No, I said L.S.D. Try to pay attention. And I made love with
someone, a professor of literature, my dream man, while I was on
it. And afterward, when I lay there, trembling with love and grati-
tude, he turned to me and told me—*told* me—that he had used the
hallucinatory effect of the drug to transform me into his physical

ideal. Even what I had become wasn't perfect, wasn't enough, he could never see, touch, taste, grasp, take, love *me*.

FAG (*Who has listened with patience rather than interest*).

Where exactly was this party you were at tonight?

STUD

What does it matter? Can't you see what I'm trying to say is that they're all alike? That's how all those businessmen were looking at me tonight—that's why they needed the candlelight and the drugs and the darkness—to blur me into some baby-doll ideal. It didn't matter to them that I'd worked those damned weights for years, putting on muscles like make-up, that I'd broadened my chest and deepened my voice and made myself into a sex-god sacrifice for them. They had to dim the lights and put on their damned Couregges sunglasses—

(FAG *touches his*)

—until I became even more vague and generalized. They didn't appreciate my ... plastic surgery ... any more than they had my writing. No amount of work could make them love me—*me*!—under the brawn and the blond, the puce and the Nile, the pullover and the hip-huggers ...

(FAG *has become galvanized with growing suspicion*)

... Even if I had these off they would still have to try to turn me into a daydream ... to worship me and not want me!

(*He rips his clothes in his frenzy*)

Oh, sweet God, please free me from this fog of flesh! I'm so tired of getting what I don't deserve!

(*The foghorns have been mounting to a terrible climax.* STUD *falls to his knees in rags, weeping.* FAG *stands trembling with excitement. Finally the foghorns fade*)

STUD (*Weak, lonely*).

Hey ... are you still there?

FAG (*Who has been groping in the wrong direction*).

Oh, yes, yes, I'm here. You ... uh ... wandered off. I could hardly hear what you were saying.

STUD

Did I? Well, I'm out of practice at writing, but I could probably condense it all for you. I'm seventeen and skinny and scrawny and nobody can love me because I'm not a big, beautiful, mindless sex god.

FAG

You're not?

(Idea)

Would you like a cigarette?

STUD *(Suddenly aware that he is half-naked in the cold).*

Yes. Yes, I would. I had some here. Must have dropped them.

(He stands and bends over, feeling the grass)

What the hell? Wet, cold grass.

(FAG clicks lighter on, searches for STUD and finds himself illuminating with the lighter nothing less than the famous Nile green ass. Clicks lighter off. Dances with glee. Restrains himself.)

FAG

Uh . . . would you like one of mine?

STUD

Where are you?

FAG

Here.

(FAG holds out cigarettes at arm's length. Stud finds it, takes one. They touch hands. FAG holds out lighter at arm's length, masking his face with his other hand. STUD pulls at cigarette hungrily, shivers.)

STUD

Thanks. Thanks a lot. What brand are these? Keep on talking, will you? I feel alone as hell.

FAG

Keep the pack if you like. They're imported.

looking for the right words).

. . have a wonderful gift for words . . . for a
d really think you were much more developed
ire someone who can write.

ore.

. Your . . . uh . . . descriptions and . . . uh . . .
imagery, are very . . . uh . . . vivid, yes, vivid.
id mind and . . . uh . . . imagination. You . . .

it's all.

nk with me. Shall I be just as frank with you?
e interested in hearing about me?

FAG

Writers are always interested in people. That's one of the most
attractive things about them.

STUD

You find that attractive? Most people don't.

FAG

Why, when I was listening to you, I felt you were saying things
I'd always felt, but couldn't articulate, express. Uh . . . I can't see a
thing. Can you?

STUD

No, nothing. God, doesn't this ever lift?

FAG

Well, I felt you were talking about *me.*

STUD

That's the highest compliment any writer could ever have.

FAG

Is it? Good! I mean, the physical description and all: huge, hefty, good-looking, all that? That party I left tonight? Well, I left to follow that boy, because ... because ...

(Inspiration)

... because he had such a compassionate face!

STUD *(Intrigued).*

When did you come in?

FAG

Oh. Oh, I had *just* come in. He didn't see me, because ... because ... because he was so busy staring at this disgusting little fairy who was masturbating on the floor, in his chic sunglasses—

(Throws them away)

and his Beatles wig—

(Throws it away)

and his Cardin suit!

(Flings jacket away)

I guess that's why he stomped out, disgusted by that little fruit! And I followed him because he looked so sensitive and intelligent. But I'm not sorry I lost him now. Not now. May I be even more honest?

STUD

What are you trying to say?

FAG

Well it's hard. I mean, one gets so used to insincere people.

STUD

I know. I know.

Fag

But I'm tired of being a big, blond, beautifully built sex god, too, like you. I mean, like the people you described. I've always wanted to meet someone like you, who could understand that, and appreciate me for myself ... even if he was just a skinny scrawny pimply kid like you.

Stud

Really?

Fag

Listen, I'm going to be even franker. I may shock you and all, but ... I don't think people should let a moment like this go—Does that sound silly to you?

Stud

Oh, God, no, not at all.

(He is sitting up now, reaching out)

Fag

I know a place just a little ways from here. I'm sure I can find it even in the dark. What I'm saying is ... will you come there with me ... now?

Stud

You sound very excited.

Fag

I've been there lots of times before. And lots of things have happened that have been ugly. But I think if I went there with someone with a beautiful soul—like you—it could make up for all those times. To go there with someone I could ... respect and admire, someone who'd appreciate me for more than just my beauty ...

(Stud has begun weeping, helplessly, happily)

Huh? What are you laughing at? Are you laughing at *me*?

Stud

No ... no ... I'm not laughing. Oh, God, I'm not laughing.

(He is on his knees, hands out, groping for Fag)

Do you mean the things you're saying?

FAG

Can you doubt me?

STUD

No, no, I can't, I don't.

(Their hands connect)

FAG

Come with me. Come with me now.

(He drags STUD *away on his knees)*

STUD

Oh, God! This is the rational world at last!

*(*FAG *drags* Stud *into the bushes as the foghorns restate their solemn, mournful theme)*

C U R T A I N

1 9 7 0 s

▭ ▪ ▭

FAIRY TALE

for Mark Giangrande

FAIRY TALE

The setting is a dressing room on the road, far underground. The room is festooned with baskets of flowers and Good Luck banners. Champagne bottles and many glasses are in evidence.

On one wall hangs an enormous poster with two huge words: "Amos Alone," and underneath in excited letters: "First solo concert!"

AMOS, a short, not particularly handsome man of about thirty, sits at his dressing table in a gorgeous bathrobe, exhausted, flushed, happy, breathing heavily, and waving at the offstage people to whom LEON, his roadie, is giving energetic farewells. LEON sports extravagant Western gear, but his speech is pure New Yorkese.

LEON *(At door).*

Yeah, goodbye. It was grand to see you, too. Yeah, he's whipped, poor baby. Terrific of you to come. We'll see y'all in New York, at the Garden? You bet. Love and kisses to the family. Take it easy. Hang loose. You flying? You don't fly? The train! I love it, yes, maybe we should, too; you can't be too careful with a one-man gold mine, ha-ha-ha-ha-ha, love you all.

(LEON closes the door, falls against it with a happy whooooosh, dusts his hands together, and smiles)

*(*Amos *raises his weary head, looks in the mirror, shudders, and releases a long pent-up sigh of relief)*

AMOS

Wow! Star city, hey?

LEON

They all came. Every one of 'em. More Grammys in that crowd than in all of Las Vegas—put together! There would be no music business if a bomb had fallen on this dressing room tonight.

AMOS

Spit!

LEON *(Hilariously playing along)*.

Oh, God!

AMOS *(Happy, teasing)*.

Spit! Spit and spin! You said a bad luck thing!

LEON

Okay, God, okay! Wow!

*(*LEON *spits on the floor three times between crossed fingers)*

AMOS

One. Two. Three. Okay, now spin in it!

LEON

Oh, Jesus God!

AMOS

Spin!

*(*LEON *spins on one foot in the spittle, three times)*

One. Two. Three.

(They fall into one another's arms, exuberant and triumphant)

LEON

We won! We won! We did it, baby! You did it! You did it, you did it, you diddledy-diddledy-did it!

(Shoves the giggling AMOS *to mirror)*

Look at yourself. Look at your sensational solo self. You did it and you did it all alone!

AMOS

I did. I really did. All alone. Me and my guitar. I haven't ever sung in front of any audience alone.

LEON

Not since you wowed us all at assembly at Erasmus High!

AMOS

Did I? I don't remember. I don't remember ever doing it, and to-night I did. Thirty-four years old!

LEON *(Brandishes "Amos Alone" album).*

They are unloading the album in a million stores tonight. It shipped double platinum!

AMOS

Double platinum. And I did it all alone.

(He suddenly collapses in LEON's *arms and shrieks in despair)*

Ah, Leon, Leon!

LEON

Ah, Amos, don't weep, darlin'.

AMOS

Oh, God, Leon, I don't want to live. I don't want to live. What's the point of living?

LEON

Baby, you're wingin'.

AMOS

I can't go to New York. I can't go anywhere. I can't ever do that again!

LEON *(Making* AMOS *sit).*

Baby, come down. Quit snivelin'. You hear me? You hear Leon? Come down. Breathe. Breathe like the doctor said. Breathe in, breathe

out, breathe in, breathe out, in, out, in, and hold it until you get
yourself centered.

(AMOS *obeys*)

Now ... you all right?

AMOS (*Lets air out*).

No! I'm not all right—

(LEON *moves to help*)

But I'm not gonna cry anymore.

LEON

Okay. Now listen. You thought you could never perform by yourself. You thought you could never perform again at all, do you
remember that? ... Answer Leon.

AMOS

Yes, God, I'm not amnesiac.

LEON

Do you remember tellin' me, just six months ago, that what you
went out there and did tonight could never, never in God's universe, be done?

(*It might appear to an unbiased observer that* LEON *is not totally
without pleasure in these dramatics*)

AMOS

Yes, I remember, I know, but, Leon—

LEON

But nothin', angel. But nothin'. What's after "but?" Rubber rooms?
Whirlpool baths? Eastern religion? Huh? Is there anything after
"but?" Anything possible?

AMOS

No, no, no.

LEON

That's a good boy. That's a best boy.

(*Glances at door*)

And a best boy always gets a reward.

AMOS *(Trying to play along).*

Aw, what reward? What have you gone and done for me now? Did you get me another classic Impala?

LEON *(I've got a secret).*

Noooooo ...

AMOS

Did you have the house in Malibu super-Dolbyed so I can record myself in the shower?

LEON

Nooooo ...

AMOS

Did you fill me up a whole motel with the Vienna Boys' Choir?

LEON *(Laughs).*

No, no. I did not. I didn't buy you anything. You got somethin' all by yourself. You did it. You got it.

AMOS

What? Did I win another prize?

LEON

Noooo. Well, yeah. What would you like more than anything in the world? Hm?

AMOS

Oh, I would like my uvula dissected so I could sing duets with myself. You gonna arrange that?

LEON

No, Amos, quit kiddin'. I mean it. What would you like most in the world to have happen?

AMOS

What is this, an interview? I would like to be a movie star, of course. Oh, God! Did we get an invite? Did we get a movie offer? Did we?

LEON

Quit foolin' around wit' me, Amos! What do you want most in the world? Answer!

AMOS

Oh, I don't know. What would I like best? You know me better than I know myself. What is it?

LEON

No, listen, Amos, I am talkin' straight wit' you. What you want most . . .

(Points dramatically at door)

. . . is waitin' right outside that door.

AMOS

Oh, no.

LEON

Now, listen to Leon, please . . . Are you goin' to be okay?

AMOS

Leon, please don't tell me what you're going to tell me.

LEON

I will, you know I will. That's because I'm your friend. That's *why* I've always been your best friend.

AMOS

Leon, I have to have a minute . . .

LEON

It's a honor to be your friend, Amos. All the world wants to be your friend. Millions and millions of strangers love and respect you, so you gotta get some sense of your own value so you can do what you have to do, do you hear me?

AMOS

You're treating me like a junky or a crazy person, like somebody that has got to be talked down!

LEON

You are not a junky or a crazy person, you are an artist, a sensitive artist, and you need someone to keep you straight, you nut!

AMOS

That's why I have you.

LEON

Not me.

AMOS

Leon—

LEON

Breathe!

AMOS

I don't wanna breathe!

LEON

Amos, I don't know what you're goin' through, because what happened to you never happened to me. There probably isn't anybody in this world that can understand you except that man out there. And I can't tell you what to do, because you're all alone at the top of the world. You go places nobody else ever goes and you come back wit' your songs. I don't know what you go through, but I know what you put me through, and I can't handle it anymore, that's the truth. I know that sooner or later you are goin' to have to deal wit' this . . .

(Points at door)

AMOS

I think it's too soon.

LEON

So wait until too late? So what happens then? He goes away?

AMOS

No, he doesn't go away. That's obvious.

LEON

So he comes in. That's obvious, too, isn't it?

AMOS

Yeah, and I go out a window first. That's obvious, too.

LEON

No windows. We're eighty feet underground.

AMOS

I didn't know I'd have to do this this soon, is all. I mean, I can do it. I can do anything, I can do this.

LEON

That's my famous Amos!

AMOS

I can see him. I can say hello.

LEON

Honey, it's more than that. And I don't know how to tell you, because even the heart can only take so much.

AMOS

Don't quote that song, please, Leon, not that one.

LEON

Okay, but it's true. There's one more thing I have to tell you, and wouldn't it be the hardest thing of all?

AMOS

God, that's from a song, too. I wrote all this before I knew I'd ever have to live it.

LEON

Right, so I don't know how to tell you this, because even you haven't taught us all to say it yet.

AMOS

So just tell me. I'm all right. I'm a survivor.... So? What?

LEON

Take a deep breath and hold it.

(AMOS *does*)

Okay. Remember you faced tonight and got through it.

(AMOS *nods, puffy-cheeked*)

Okay. It's this . . . He wants to come back.

AMOS

He—?

(Breathes frantically)

LEON

So you have what you want, Amos. Remember, you are one of the few people in the whole history of the world to have exactly what he wants. Don't say anything. Breathe if you have to. I'm goin' over to that door now and let him in. I'm over at the door now. Remember, he's goin' through it all, too. But he's never sung alone and heard the people cheer.

AMOS

He sung alone.

LEON

He flopped. Be sensible now.
(Pantomime:
LEON *reaches for the doorknob.*
AMOS *stops him with a gesture.*
LEON *starts to speak.*
AMOS *commands silence, walks slowly and with dignity to his dressing table.*
He sits calmly, fusses with his hair.
He sticks his tongue out at himself.
He strikes a pose of quiet self-command, gestures to LEON.
LEON *opens the door.*
AMOS *hides his face in his hands.*
Too late. The door is open.)

LEON

Sigh. Hello, Sphinx. You might as well come in.

(SPHINX *enters. He is tall . . . well, taller than* AMOS. *He is blond.
He is beautiful. He has been loved all his life, and always will be.
His smile tells you where his nickname came from.*)

SPHINX

Hi, Leon. How are Sylvia and the kids?

LEON

I'm goin' out. Will you two guys need anything?

SPHINX

No, thanks, Leon.

LEON

I'll stay out until you call me.

SPHINX

Yes, Leon.

(LEON *exits.* SPHINX *closes the door. On the back of it hangs a gaudy
coat of* AMOS's. SPHINX *strokes it, turns and looks at* AMOS, *whose
face is still hidden.* SPHINX *leans against the door, casually.*)

SPHINX

Hi.

AMOS (*Mumbles incoherently behind his hands*).

SPHINX

I know you don't. But I don't know what to say, either, so it
doesn't matter.

AMOS (*Mumbles incoherently behind his hands*).

SPHINX

I can look at *you*. I love to look at *you*.

AMOS (*Mumbles incoherently*).

SPHINX

Yes, and you ought to know what *I'm* going to say, but you never,

never do. Amos, I'm sorry I left and I'd like to come back and sing with you.

AMOS *(Uncovers mouth, eyes still covered).*
I almost died.

SPHINX
Me, too, but I didn't . . . Did you?

AMOS *(laughs behind his hands).*
Don't make me laugh.

SPHINX
You know, you're wasting a perfectly good mirror.

AMOS *(Uncovers eyes, but looks at his lap).*
Do you know something funny? I didn't even wonder if you'd come here tonight. It didn't even occur to me to wonder.

SPHINX
That's what I thought.

AMOS *(Looks up at SPHINX in mirror, looks away).*
I don't mean that I took it for granted. I didn't mean that.

SPHINX
I know.

AMOS
I mean I never thought of it at all. Of you at all. That way.

SPHINX *(First sigh of fatigue).*
I understand.

AMOS
I think about you.

SPHINX
Yes.

AMOS
I think about you all the time.

SPHINX
Yes.

AMOS
But not of you being *here*.

SPHINX
I wouldn't have not been here for anything in the world. . . . Can I come over there?

AMOS
You're bigger than I am. I can't stop you.

SPHINX *(Walks to table, stands behind* AMOS*)*.
I'm over here now.

AMOS *(Sloooowly lifts his eyes to mirror)*.
Hello.

SPHINX *(Puts his hands on* AMOS*'s shoulders)*.
Now we look just like the cover of our first album. We look just like the cover of "Fairy Tale."

AMOS
No, I look older.

SPHINX
I'm older, too.

AMOS
No, you don't. Look it.

SPHINX
Then you're still in love with me.

AMOS *(Spins to face* SPHINX, *embraces his hips)*.
Yes!

SPHINX
That's going to make this a whole lot harder for you.

AMOS *(Lets him go)*.

Sphinx! How can you just say that?

SPHINX

Ah, Amos, we have to talk.

AMOS

Honey, baby, I don't know if I can.

SPHINX

Sure we can.

(Pulls up a chair)

We have to, after all, don't we now?

AMOS

I don't know what's happening. I haven't got my bearings. I don't know what's going on inside me.

SPHINX

Ah, I do. Take my hands.

*(*AMOS *does)*

I'm sorry to come back and hurt you. But I don't think it hurts any more than when I wasn't here, does it?

AMOS

That's like asking whether it hurts more to lose your leg or to see it lying in front of you!

*(*AMOS *is struggling to free his hands)*

SPHINX

Ah, God, baby, that's what it's like for me, too.

AMOS

Then where have you *been?*

(Gets hands free, turns away) .

Oh, I don't want to know!

SPHINX *(Whirls* AMOS *back around)*.

Sure you do. You know, anyway.

AMOS *(Covers ears with hands).*

No, I don't, no, I don't, no I don't.

SPHINX *(Calmly).*

I went off with another man and I made movies with him, and they didn't work out, so I came back to see if you want us to sing together again. It can be said.

AMOS *(Removes hands from ears).*

I don't know why people put their hands over their ears; you can hear with your hands over your ears.

SPHINX

People put their hands over their ears when there's a loud, loud noise . . . to protect the sensitive parts from the shock.

AMOS

That sounds like lines from a goddamned song.

SPHINX

I wanted to cover my ears tonight when you sang the old songs. And I wanted to cover them when you sang the new songs you wrote without me. The old songs and the new songs hurt me just about the same.

AMOS

And when the applause came? When they all stood up?

SPHINX

It was hard for you to bow without me being there and us holding hands. It was hard to take a bow alone.

AMOS *(Rises and walks away, angry).*

How did you *know* that?

SPHINX *(Shrugs).*

Everyone's the same about love.

AMOS

That sounds like a line from a song.

(Improvises tunes)

"Everyone's the same about love." "The old songs and the new songs hurt me just about the—" Everything you say sounds like lines from a song!

SPHINX

This *is* going to be a lot harder for you than for me.

AMOS

Why for?

SPHINX

Because you're still in love with me—

AMOS

What?

SPHINX

So it's going to be tougher going for you—

AMOS

How can you—

SPHINX

But I'm here to help you any way I can—

AMOS

How can you just—

SPHINX

And I know what you're going through.

AMOS

Sphinx! How can you just *say* that?

SPHINX

I can always say anything to you. Remember?

AMOS

Oh, God, this is all so ... so ... so—

SPHINX

Real, darling. It's all so real. It's funny—

AMOS

Funny? Roast a baby!

SPHINX

I'm not used yet to being stronger than you. You were always the strong one. Makes me feel better. I've felt so weak since we split up.

AMOS

Since you *left*.

SPHINX

You weren't there anymore to take care of me.

AMOS

You were always stronger than me. I'm a mess!

SPHINX

Honey, from the moment we met, you were always so strong.

AMOS

Hey, you came up to me.

SPHINX

From the moment I met you.

AMOS

You actually came up to me.

SPHINX

I was so shy.

AMOS

I was. I wanted to talk to you forever.

SPHINX

You were that kid who played the guitar so good.

AMOS
You came up to me.
(Wonder in his voice)

SPHINX *(Warm humor in his).*
I finally got the nerve.

AMOS
I never would. I was watching you all through the ninth grade.

SPHINX
I saw you staring.

AMOS
You looked right over me.

SPHINX
I thought you thought I was funny-looking.

AMOS
I told Leon. You were the most beautiful thing I ever saw.

SPHINX
And then I heard you playing your guitar.

AMOS
I thought you were coming to beat me up.

SPHINX
I had to talk to you.

AMOS
I couldn't move.

SPHINX
There was just one thing I wanted to do.

AMOS
Right there on the playground?

SPHINX

I only wanted to touch your old guitar.

AMOS

You could have touched my liver if you wanted to.

SPHINX

To see if it was still vibrating.

AMOS

It was. It is. I thought I was going to die.

SPHINX

And did you?

AMOS

No fair making me laugh.

SPHINX

I *thought* it was your guitar I wanted to touch.

AMOS

You asked me if I had any songs of my own.

SPHINX

And you did.

AMOS

No, I didn't.

SPHINX

You always say that. You played lots of your songs for me.

AMOS

I didn't. Did I?

SPHINX

You played songs for me for days.

AMOS

I don't remember.

SPHINX
Wonderful songs.

AMOS
I don't remember writing songs before you.

SPHINX
One of us has to remember.

AMOS
I never *really* wrote any songs before I met you.

SPHINX
I know.

AMOS
I know you know.
(They have moved into a gentle embrace)

SPHINX
You turned everything I said into a song.

AMOS
It's that way you have of speaking.

SPHINX
It's that way you have of listening to me.

AMOS
Everything you say sounds like a song.

SPHINX
Not really.

AMOS
It always did. It always will.

SPHINX
That's because you're still in love with me.

AMOS

That sounds like you're not.

SPHINX

It sounds like that because that's how it is.

AMOS *(Pulls away, almost covers ears).*

Sphinx ...

SPHINX

I love you. How could I ever not love you? Where would I be? Amos, where would the world be without you?

AMOS

I'm nothing without *you.*

SPHINX

Honey, that may be. That may very well be. But it looks like you're fine without me—

(Indicates "Amos Alone" poster)

But, of course, we're never going to find out.

AMOS *(Back in SPHINX's arms).*

No, no, we won't.

SPHINX

Because we're never going to be without each other.

AMOS *(Pulls away).*

Hey, what if I don't want you back?

SPHINX

Whether I come back or not, we're together. We've been together too long. I know it, you know it, it's very well-known.

AMOS

God! Everything you say sounds like a—

SPHINX *(First anger).*

That's because you always make me say everything! That's why you always insisted on putting my name on the songs!

AMOS
Nobody knows.

SPHINX *(Grabs him, makes him face the poster).*
I think they know *now*, Amos!
(Relents)
Oh, God!
(Spins AMOS *to face mirror. Strikes "Fairy Tale" pose again)*
Look, look. The cover of "Fairy Tale."

AMOS
But I'm so *old*.

SPHINX
We sold more copies of that album than anybody ever sold before!

AMOS
Everybody loved you.

SPHINX
Supermarkets, elevators, jukeboxes, radios rang with your songs.

AMOS
Rang with *our* songs.

SPHINX
The unlikeliest people sang them. Andy Williams!

AMOS
Not like you did, we did.

SPHINX
We were the most famous gay couple that ever had existed.

AMOS
Nobody knew.

SPHINX
The gay kids knew. They never had heroes like us before.

AMOS

There was never anybody like us.

SPHINX

Anybody like you.

AMOS

I couldn't have done it without you.

(He tears "Amos Alone" poster from wall)

SPHINX

Well, we'll never know.

AMOS

We've been apart so long.

SPHINX

Only a year.

AMOS

Only!

SPHINX

You see, Amos, that's the difference between us. You're still in the fairy tale. Whereas I'm going on real time now. Real time is very hard. It's very different. But you'll get used to it. And when you do, it's better, because it's real.

AMOS

It was very hard writing the new songs.

SPHINX

They're wonderful songs.

AMOS

Some.

SPHINX

Most.

Amos

Everybody kept saying, "You need three more songs for an album."

Sphinx

Ah, God, Amos, I'm sorry I left you alone.

Amos

I had to write without you there with me.

Sphinx

I'm really sorry.

Amos

Then why did you? How could you? Why did you went away and left me alone?

Sphinx

I fell in love with someone else—

Amos *(Puts hands over Sphinx's mouth)*.

Sphinx, no.

Sphinx *(Removes hands)*.

That's all.

Amos

All? That's all? All?

Sphinx

That's what happened. I'd never lie to you.

Amos

And you went off to be a movie star and left me all alone.

Sphinx

Yes.

Amos

And you failed.

SPHINX
Yes.

AMOS
And now you come back like nothing's changed.

SPHINX
I've changed.

AMOS
Everything's changed.

SPHINX
Yes.

AMOS
It was you changed it.

SPHINX
Yes.

AMOS
Well, I am doing fine on my own.
   (Waves poster)
I don't know if I need you anymore.

SPHINX
You know you do.

AMOS
What do you know? What do I need you for?

SPHINX
Because everything I say sounds like a song.

AMOS
You're scared, that's what!

SPHINX
Yes.

AMOS

You went out there without me and you couldn't take it.

SPHINX

Yes.

AMOS

And now you're scared and you come crawling back like everything's the same—

SPHINX

No.

AMOS

Well, let me tell you something, *Spencer!* I did pretty well standing up out there alone tonight, and I got a record shipping double platinum tomorrow, and it's chock-full of some of the best work little Amos has done yet, and I even learned to breathe! So don't come ambling back on the assumption that I can't get along without you, because I have pretty well conclusively demonstrated that I can. I can write, I can sing, I can perform pretty damned well all on my own!

SPHINX

But, Amos, do you want to?

AMOS *(Flees into* SPHINX*'s open arms).*

Nooooooooooooooo! You're what I want, you're what I need, you're what I do it all for, it's nothing without you, I'm just another dumb pop star, a diamond a dozen, there's ten million people out there clawing and tugging at me, and you're the only real thing that ever mattered. Why did you go away, why did you leave me, why did you ever come back? I just only want to hold onto you.

(They squeeze each other until you'd think juice would come out. They relax. AMOS *pulls away, wiping tears from his eyes.)*

You can come back if you want to.

SPHINX

Oh, I do. I miss you all the time.

AMOS

So just ... don't say you're not in love with me anymore.

SPHINX

Oh, Amos I'm not. But it doesn't really matter. There'll come a time when you're not in love with me, and I'll have to bear up under that. I'm so used to you being in love with me. We had something very special ... boy, I didn't know. We found each other very young and we were never ever apart. We were a fairy tale, and we were true, and we showed the whole world how it could be if two men were let to love each other. Then I made a mistake and the fairy tale was over. It is over.

AMOS

It doesn't have to be?

SPHINX

Sure it does. Didn't you ever notice, fairy tales are short? Did you wonder why? I figured it out. It's because if they go on too long they turn into horror stories. Amos, you're in love with me, and I'm not with you, but I'm here, and I'll be here, and I'm your friend. I love and understand you, and I'll be here to help you get to the other side. I'm a little ahead of you, and that makes me seem strong. But I'll lose your love, and then I'll need you to be *my* friend. I seem strong, and then you'll seem strong, and then if we're lucky and honest and wise, we'll *be* strong, each on our own. And then, I suspect, we'll laugh and talk about it, many a night, laugh and talk about it all night long. And we'll go on.

AMOS

Sphinx, why *did* you leave me?

SPHINX *(Sees that it must be said, sighs, sits down;* AMOS *sits at his feet).*

Why ... did I ... leave you?

(He strokes AMOS*'s hair)*

Once upon a time ... there was a land where fairies had to hide. They had to become invisible, or disguise themselves as other kinds of creatures, or find secret places no one else knew about. And so they became legendary, fabulous creatures. And so they began to think about themselves. They were strange, they were different, they were myths and phantoms and dreams. And then there arose among them a fantastic magician, who had the power to cast powerful spells. And he slowly became able to walk abroad among the real people, and there one day he met an enchanted prince—

Amos

—With golden hair.

Sphinx

—With golden hair. And he said to the prince, "Let us go forth and break the evil spell that binds our people." And so they went forth, with the magician spreading his magical music far and wide and near, and indeed the fairies began to be released. And, wonder of wonders, they discovered as they met the world and each other in their true likenesses, that they were only ordinary people, not special, not strange, not mysterious, not odd at all. And it was very hard to understand that, to give up that special feeling, to come slowly, ever so slowly, down to earth. But the magical musician—

Amos

—and his beautiful prince—

Sphinx

—and his beautiful prince kept spreading the magic spells, and helped them all. Their magic was like a net that gently lowered the frightened fairies to the ground, until they had learned to stand on their own two feet. And then one day, the prince—

Amos

—beautiful prince—

Sphinx

—the prince met an evil magician.

AMOS

No.

SPHINX

Yes. And the evil magician told the prince that the prince was magical, too, and could weave magical spells all on his own. So he left the musical magician and went away. And he learned very quickly that he . . . he was only ordinary, too.

AMOS

Sphinx—

SPHINX

Ssshhhh. So he found out he was real. But he also found out that when you are real, then you can feel real love. And he only felt it for the magician he'd left. And so he came back. For real.

AMOS

Oh, Sphinx. I could only live because you thought I was so wonderful.

SPHINX

Wonderful? Amos, I think you're more wonderful now than I ever thought before. I think you're *really* wonderful. Come on, now. I've got a car waiting. Let's go back to your hotel.

AMOS *(As* SPHINX *helps him change into the gaudy coat).*

Are you going to stay with me?

SPHINX

Oh, I am, I am.

AMOS

You're wrong, you know.

SPHINX

You're getting better. You used to say I was never wrong.

AMOS

You're wrong about one thing. You're not ordinary. You never were. You couldn't have been and still have made what happened,

happen. I'm going to show you—not just tonight, although I'm
certainly going to show you tonight—I'm going to show you just
how wonderful you are.

SPHINX

Just how wonderful I am?

AMOS

Yes.

SPHINX *(Slyly)*.

You're going to show me just how wonderful I *really* am?

AMOS *(Caught)*.

Yes.

SPHINX

Oh, Amos, my dearest darling; I hope so.
(They embrace)
(SPHINX opens the door)

All right, Leon, you can come in now.

LEON *(Enters)*.

Hi, boys. You two make everything up okay?

AMOS

Huh?

SPHINX

Yes, we did, Leon. Thank you very much.

LEON

Well, that's news. I mean, that's good news.

SPHINX

Yes, Leon. Both of the above.
(SPHINX and AMOS exit)

LEON

Yessiree. Yessirree. That's news. That's good news.
(He sees "Amos Alone" poster, picks it up)

Hey, this'll be a collector's item. Two legends back together again!
(He turns out the light and exits, closing the door behind him)

C U R T A I N

1 9 8 0 s

◼▬◼·◼▬◼

POUF POSITIVE

for Elaine Gold

POUF POSITIVE

The setting is Robin's *apartment on an upper floor of a building in New York's Greenwich Village. It features everything a retentive queen would have acquired living in New York from 1967 through 1987.*

Posters are layered on the walls. The earliest are vivid old movie posters, then pop art, some Beardsley, some personality posters of Kennedy and Che, some psychedelic rock and religion, some gay power, some gay theater, Evita and Annie, disco stars, opera, est, Dolly Parton, and finally flyers for AIDS benefits. In every layer are photos torn from increasingly explicit male porn magazines.

A clothes rack holds garments ranging from fluffy sweaters and chinos to jeans and ponchos, gowns and boas, glittered jump suits, rhinestoned T-shirts, yellow rain slickers covered in graffiti, military uniforms, djellebas, and finally a few conservative business suits.

A revolving wire paperback rack holds hundreds of volumes. A shelf holds a complex stereo system and innumerable records and tapes. Many dead plants hang from the ceiling, along with a dusty crepe-paper piñata in the shape of Miss Piggy, and a mobile, whose dangling elements are a star, a dollar sign, a peace sign, a hypodermic, a gold record, a muscle man, a Rolls Royce, a computer, and Tinker Bell.

Propped up in a wicker peacock chair is Robin, *an emaciated man of about forty. He wears pajamas and has a coverlet over his lap. Beside him is a table covered with sickroom paraphernalia, flowers in a vase, condolence cards, a telephone, and an unactivated answering machine.*

Through a window beside him, we see a church steeple and an early morning sky.

At rise, ROBIN *is writing something on a pad across his knees.*

ROBIN *(With a final pencil flourish).*
There! That just about says it!
(He tears it off, weakly, folds it, and looks for a place to put it, deciding finally on his pajama pocket)
Now. Let's see if we can still manage a limerick.
(He writes and speaks)
There once was a Manhattan queen—
(Phone rings. He ignores it.)
—With nothing that she hadn't seen—
(Phone rings)
—'Til they said, "No charades."
(Phone rings. He grows annoyed.)
"You're a person with AIDS."
(Phone rings)
"Abandon all plans for the screen?"
(Phone rings)
"You'd better put down that marine?"
(Phone rings)
"Don't subscribe to a new magazine?"
(Phone rings)
Mom didn't turn on your machine.
(Answers phone)
Okay, I can't make little songs out of my great sorrows;
I may as well talk to you.
But be advised:
If you're calling to tell me *you've* got it,

Save both our breaths.
Just say, "ditto,"
And leave me to my beads.

Oh, Bob!
Of course you haven't got it;
Who'd give it to you?
Except a good-hearted U.S.O. girl like me?
And *we* were 'way back in the sixties,
When the word AIDS was preceded
By the words American Military.

How am I?
Well, when I think of what I've got, I feel like shit,
But when I think of how I got it, I can't complain.
How are you?

I know you've called.
I hate those "Twilight Zone" episodes where people install phones
in their coffins,
So I haven't been answering mine.
This exception is not because I still love you,
But because I've written some hilarious last words.
I want someone literate listening, in case I croak
While Mom and Sis are out at morning mass.
They're here to identify the body—
Which millions could do in the dark—
And to pray for the soul,
The mind being unknown to them.
You, I presume, have called to glean piquant detail
On what it's like to die as I have lived,
A sociosexualogical statistic.
I know you writers, you're life's hungry men.
Well, here's a fairly poignant paradox for your next play:
I came home from a rally for gay rights
Only to learn I have the great gay wrong.
Wait, that isn't a paradox, is it? It's an irony.
It's an irony; it's one of life's little ironies,
Like Anita Bryant turning out to be right.

Bob, don't bother to answer back.
Anything said to me at this point
Might as well be written on a decomposing squash.
The brain goes first, you know—
Except for the portions dedicated to pain,
Which are apparently immune.

"Do I need anything?" Oh, how droll.
Wait, I may have just enough strength for a comeback to that:
No, I don't need anything. I already have
Cancer, pneumonia, and my mother at my side—
All the things that make life worth leaving. How's that?

Come over? Be serious! I look like Mia Farrow, halfway through
Rosemary's Baby.
I want you to remember me as the Botticelli flower child I once was.
God!
I was the prettiest queen that ever paraded for peace
And now I'm something that needs to be burnt after death.
I was pretty, wasn't I?
. . . Bob?
All right, smart ass, you can answer that one,
But think before you speak.

   (A chime rings)

Well, saved by the cliche; aren't *you* the lucky one!
That's the church bell.
One stroke means it's seven-thirty.
At eight o'clock it's a David O. Selznick production up here.
And Mom and Sis will come crawling upstairs on their knees,
Muttering rosaries.
So I'm yours 'til eight o'clock or the end of time,
Whichever comes first.
Oh, wait; what's that couplet by old A. E. Houseman:
"And he shall hear the stroke of eight
And not the stroke of nine."
About the condemned man in *his* cell?
Hah!
Condemned for not being condomed!
The wit and wisdom of the living dead.

Like it? I leave it to you. Want anything else? Records? Tapes?
The history of Western music from Mahalia to Michael Jackson?
I want to give it all away
Before some fool plays disco at my funeral
And the record gets stuck
And nobody can tell
And the service goes on forever!
But I'm being negative.
Wanna hear some positive funeral jokes?
I want to be freeze-dried and cut in half
And made into ballerina plaques.
No, actually, I insist on being cremated;
It's my last chance to get my ashes hauled.
No, actually, I want my ashes mixed with greasepaint
And used as blackface for Diana Ross drags.
Then I want my Mastercard and all my I.D.
Clipped together
And flung to the cutest kid in Sheridan Square!
And I don't want you reading any of your crappy monologues,
Or mine.
I already cremated all of my so-called works.

Oh, shut up. I was not a real writer.
Which you, of course, are; I apologize for that base canard.
All I had was a knack for cute coffee-table metaphors, like:
"Joan Collins is as vulgar as Christmas in Mexico!"
Or remember I called that nervous friend of yours,
"As delicate as *The Glass Menagerie* in Braille."
And of one of my own true loves—not you—I was heard to quip:
"His cock is like cake, his balls are like bells,
But his ass is like ice."

Thanks.
Wait, those aren't metaphors; they're similes.
That's me: Simile Dickinson.
Forgive the low level of repartee at this end.
I haven't been reading anything except condolence cards.
A pixieish fellow P.W.A. sent one that says,
"What do you give the man who has everything?"

I'm designing one to be sent by well-meaning, helpless friends like
you.
It shows a quadruple amputee, saying,
"I'm behind you one hundred percent."
And, of course, Mom has been reading to me.

Oh, Shirley Maclaine's latest volume, what else?
Shirley claims we pay in each next life
For our sins in the last one.
Well, Shirl, girl, we've streamlined the process this time.
Your up-to-date pervert is dying in the fast lane.

No, I'm not going back into the hospital.
I abhor the term, *legally alive*.
God, think of the great men who have nibbled on me,
And now I'm nothing but a snack for a virus:
Something that can't even decide if it's an animal or a plant.
Let me tell you, it's no picnic *being* one.

Bob, there's nothing medical science can do:
AIDS is the gift that keeps on giving.
My luck:
I got this sweet Indian doctor, who kept
Folding and unfolding his eyeglasses like a Rubik's Cube.
He asked very shyly if he could take blood,
Urine, snot, stool, semen, and saliva specimens.
I said, "Sure; then can we do what *I* like?"
Oh, and I used one of *your* lines on the poor, sweet sap.
He very delicately informed me
There was a lot less chance of getting it
If one had been "Wot dey call a 'topman.' "
I couldn't resist it.
I said, "Doc, I've always been a topman;
You can get it further up you that way!"
Then the diagnosis came up "Bingo!"
He warned me to watch out for the depression
That *often* accompanies a diagnosis of AIDS.
So I said, with a show of great relief:
"AIDS! Oh, doctor, thank God; I thought you said, 'Age!' "

You know my motto:
Brighten the coroner where you are.
I tried to make up by offering to be a subject
For any cute tricks that science might want to try.
And he said,
"Mister Wood, we cannot use you as an experimental animal,"
And I told him,
"Doc, I'm an effeminate queer;
I've never been used as anything else!"

Except by you, Bob, yes, we know that, we were truly in love.
That was love, wasn't it? No wonder it went out of style.
No, no, I'm sorry, what you said is true:
When you fucked me over that tenement bannister
With the Day-Glo peace signs flaking off the walls,
It *was* the balcony scene of the sixties.
Christ, I used to be so clever; now I'm reduced to quoting you.
I was clever.
When I was just a little girl in East Bay, California,
I noticed that "East Bay" was pig Latin for "beast."
But I knew I had found my niche when I realized
That "Alice Faye" was pig Latin for "phallus."

Yes, isn't that good?
You think we can interest the virus in 1930s musicals
And it'll turn queer and stop reproducing?
Scratch that; you have to be born to royalty.
That's how that lovely old 1940s closet queen
Who brought me out used to put it: "Born to royalty?"
He'd spot some hunky number and lean over to me
And whisper, "Do you think *he* was born to royalty?"
Meaning was he a queen.
"Born to royalty." Sigh. God knows I was.
Twelve years old, I rummaged through the biggest
Country-western record barn in Central California
And came up with the only Marlene Dietrich album on the West
Coast.
You have to be born with that instinct.
And all by my little lonesome I discovered Walt Whitman,

And Aubrey Beardsley, and dying my bangs with lemon juice,
And ordering everything a size small,
And outlining my eyes with ball-point pen
So when the boys made me cry, they wouldn't see anything running.
When my age became the socially conscious "We Generation,"
I had to fight for my right to riot in pink high-heels.
And when we o.d.'d on politics
And became the "Me Generation,"
I drove to New York on a lavender motorcycle
After using my last sunshine acid to spike the communion wine!

No. I should have. I could have been Jimmy Jones.
I could have been a contender.
Instead of a drab example of the "De-Generation,"
Turned into a serving of sushi for a flock of plankton!
But let's not talk about me when I'm gone.
Where was I anyway; oh, yes:
We're-born-that-way, we're-part-of-nature's-plan. That riff.
Well, it's trite but it's true.
Where would the world be without its fairies?
Well, we may be about to find out, mayn't we now?
And you, you've been too ugly for a decade
For anyone to fuck with, you'll live to see it:
A world without fairies.
Bloomingdale's, of course, will have to close.
There will be no girl singers to speak of
And speak of and speak of.
Whole strains of ferns and poodles will become extinct.
Plaid shirts will be marked down to three ninety-five in memoriam.
Of course, fairies have been dying out
Since the seventies Marlboro-macho movement.
If I live 'til noon, I'll never understand the clones,
Trying to look like the bullies that beat us up in the schoolyard.
They're living proof—wherever that term still applies—
You don't have to learn to be gay;
You have to learn to act straight—
Which may be the origin of the verb "to ape"!

Thank you!
Why, if it hadn't been for a few effeminate holdouts like me,
The color beige might have vanished from the face of the earth!
Ah, God! Ah, God! Ah, God!

(He grips his abdomen in pain, breathes hard, finally speaks)

Well, give yourself a gold star; you noticed.
Yes, Bob, I'm tiring myself out.
I'm not having an experience I care to prolong.
Remember those fantasies of attending your own funeral?
It isn't as much fun as we thought it would be.
Stay on the line; those snappy last words may be imminent.

Hah!
It's my party and I'll die if I want to!

I'm sorry. I'm being cruel. What a way to go.
Look, you're okay, I'm not okay, okay? Okay.
I'm dying. Everybody dies
Except for two unconfirmed reports from Bethlehem and Transylvania.
Why does this take my generation by such surprise?
Did they think we were all just going to go into reruns?
Wouldn't you think any queen would be glad
To learn she's about to lose *all* her weight, forever?
Must one go through the five official stages?
What are those five stages again:
"Anger, denial, bargaining, depression, and acceptance."
Well, back up: here comes my acceptance speech.
"I am now and I have always been a flaming faggot,
Responsible for style in its every manifestation.
I have my own five steps:
Flippancy, sentimentality, sarcasm, camp, and smut.
Those got me through life, and, deity damn it,
They'll get me through death!"
Now shut up or I'll stop loving you.
I expected you to write something to make me live in infamy,
Like Shakespeare promised his poor Elizabethan pushover:

"Not marble nor the gilded monuments
Of princes shall outlive this powerful rhyme."
Wellllllllll,
As it turned out,
The gilded monuments of princes are major tourist attractions,
And nobody knows who the hell the sonnets were written for,
Buuuuuuut—

Oh, don't *cry*.
I love you.
You're brilliant.
That was a base canard.
You're a wonderful writer
I am less than all that dust upon your laurels.
You're probably the greatest living gay playwright.
Or with any luck soon will be.

Look, how's this for comfort?
We were the last two white people ever to fall in love.
That oughta rate some space in the "Whatever Became Of?" books.
And there are no challengers on the horizon.
How can anybody fall in something as awful as love
When they're being careful?
Before my condition started warranting quarantine,
I knew two kids:
Lovers, into safe sex, monogamous out of terror.
One night they were each jerking themselves off
While fucking the other—with vibrators—And one of them's arms
got tired, so he switched hands,
And his lover hops out of bed, screaming,
"You switched hands!
You might have got some of your precum on your fingers
And it might crawl up the vibrator into me!
Are you trying to kill me?"
Naked, except for rubber gloves and a banana-flavored condom,
With an electric dildo still revolving in his ass.
Not what one would call "love's first, fine, careless rapture,"
Now is it?

Oh, *don't*.
You're right, you're always right, yes, yes, of course,
Love will survive.
They couldn't kill it with those purple hair-do's,
They can't kill it with a plague.
Boys will fall in love with each other's earlobes
If all else should fail.
Because it was never really about sex, was it?
It was about love?

Yes, I know you did.

Yes, I know you do.

Yes, I do, too.

I'm sorry we broke up, too. I was a fool.
No, wait, maybe you were the fool. How did we break up?
You told me we had to cool it for a week because you caught crabs
And I thought it was a lie because you didn't love me,
And I took up with that jailbait street meat for revenge
And you went off in a huff to save world drama, yes,
I thought I remembered it being about love.
Well, and looky here now where we are.
I love you.
You love me.
We're having a deathbed reconciliation fadeout.
That oughta satisfy two students of *montage*.
Dear Lord, I'm suffering like a living thing.
Sex may be safe, but love never is.

 (A church bell rings)

Ah, saved from the fate worse than—

 (Looks out window)

Lemme look. Yeah, there's Mom and Sis, rushing from judgment.

 (Bell)

I can see the church and the sky
And the old International Stud Bar.

(Bell)

No, fool, it's a restaurant now like everything else.
How did they clean that back room?

(Bell)

Probably poured polyurethane
To level the ruts left by my knees.

(Bell)

No, don't call again.
Use that new phone-sex service.
It promises troll-free calls.

(Bell)

If you have to do something, write me a funny AIDS play.
Sure you can.

(Bell)

It's the biggest joke played on us since sex itself—
And with the longest punch line.

(Bell)

I don't want you to call.
If God wanted us to be friends with our old lovers,
He wouldn't have made them such creeps.
Goodbye. I love you. Shut up.

> *(Hangs up. Feels for the folded paper in his pajama pocket, takes it out, unfolds it, reads it aloud.)*

"At least I'll never have to hear the term *Life-style* again."

C U R T A I N

Untold Decades was first produced *en toto* by the Glines at The Producers Club, February 17, 1988. John Glines and Larry Bussard were executive producers, Bill Repicci was associate producer. Tracy Dedrickson designed lights and Don Newcomb was costume consultant. The cast consisted of Mark Cole as "Man" and John Wuchte as "Ralph"; Charles Carson as "John-Bo," Jeffrey J. Allbright as "Casdale," Todd Lewey as "Ray," and Joseph Zimmerman as "Aegis"; Charles Carson as "Bob," Eddie Cobb as "Bill," and Edmond Ramage as "Reverend Lawson"; Tommy Brooks as "Edgar," John Speredakos as "Brad," and Richard Reid as "Curtis"; Jeffrey Herbst as "Stud" and Eddie Cobb as "Fag"; Mark Nadler as "Leon," Herman Lademann as "Amos," and Tom Brangle as "Sphinx"; and Terry Talley as "Robin." The plays were directed respectively by William Castleman, Charles Edward Harvey, Vincent Gugleotti, Jr., Charles Catanese, Peter Pope, Michael Meyerson, and the author. James Merillat did incidental music and an adaptation of "Cigarette" for the 20s play, for which Lisa Mando did costumes. Billy Rook and Buddy Barkalow stage managed. During the run, "Fairy Tale" was replaced by "Sit-Com," in which Scott Cargle played "Ezra," Richard Reid "Ron," and Chris Holland "Doug," against a painting by Patrick Angus. The author directed.

"20s, 30s, 40s" was staged as a reading by Bill Hunt for Gay Performances in New York, with Richard Stack as "Man," Scott Cargle as "Ralph," Brian O'Sullivan as "John-Bo," Owen Wilson as "Casdale," Scott Cargle as "Ray," Patrick Donnelly as "Aegis," Richard Stack as "Bob Boseman," Owen Wilson as "Bill Batchelor," and Max Brandt as "Reverend Lawson." Don Barrington, Christian Mountain, and Michael van Atta produced; Dennis Walsh stage managed; Nancy Miller designed sound; Dennis Palante ran lights and sound.

"50s, 60s, 70s, 80s" was produced in Hollywood at the Fifth Estate Theatre by "Smitty." The author directed, and set construction was by William Houck. Larry Joe Evans was "Edgar," Don Paul was "Brad," Michael Harrington was "Captain Curtis," Benjamin Wilson was "Stud," Sherwood Scott (later David Gregory) was "Fag," Scott Belyea was "Leon," Gary Cusano was "Amos," Mitch Beckloff was "Sphinx," Rory Maloney was "Ron," Randy Noojin was "Jim," and Michael Taylor was "Doug."

"50s, 60s, 70s, 80s" was first produced by Stonewall Repertory Theater in New York in 1983. Billy Cunningham directed. "Brad," was played by David Friedlander, "Edgar," by Audie McDonald, "Curtis," by Larry Hough, "Stud," by Bruce Nozick, "Fag," by Quinton Wiles, "Amos," by Tom Starace, "Sphinx," by Alex Tolstoi, "Leon," by Doug Bolston, "Jim," by Michael Pinzone, "Ron," by Alex Danyluk, "Doug," by Richard J. Connery. Michael Pritchard was Executive Producer, Evan Senreich, Artistic Director.

"40s" was produced in New York at Elaine Gold's Corner Loft Studio as part of the one hundreth performance gala for "Blue is for Boys." Gerry Grant was "Bill," Jon Roger Clark was "Bob," and Edmond Ramage was "Reverend Lawson."

"40s" was produced by Phil Willkie for the James White Review at Whittier Park Center in Minneapolis. Robert Patrick played "Bill," Doug Anderson played "Bob," and David Lindahl played "Reverend Lawson."

"40s" was filmed by Vic Burner in Pasadena, California, with Michael Gerard as "Bill," Randall Ulmer as "Bob," and Jim Aar as "Reverend Lawson."

"50s" was produced by Safe Sex Players in Austin, directed by Doug Dyer, with Edgar Brown as "Edgar," Danny Medina as "Brad," and Ricardo Comer as "Captain Curtis."

"Fog" premiered at Norman Hartman's Old Reliable Theatre Tavern, New York, in February 1969. Bill Haislip was "Stud," Jeffrey Herman was "Fag." The author directed and Eric Concklin designed lights.

"Sit-Com" (the original "80s" piece) premiered in Minneapolis at the Out-and-About Theatre. Richard Rehse directed.

"Pouf Positive" premiered at the Dramatic Risks Benefit at R.A.P.P. Arts Center, New York, in 1987, coordinated by Ozzie Rodriguez. Terry Talley played "Robin." The author directed. Mark Grant Waren produced.

The actors appearing in the photos (from left to right) in this edition of *Untold Decades* are:
1920s: John Wuchte, Mark Cole; 1930s: Jeffrey J. Allbright, Todd Lewey, Joseph Zimmerman, Charles Carson; 1940s: Eddie Cobb, Charles Carson; 1950s: Tommy Brooks (kneeling), John Speredakos, Richard Reid; 1960s: Eddie Cobb, Jeffrey Herbst; 1970s: Scott Cargle, Johnny Randall; 1980s: Terry Talley.

ABOUT THE AUTHOR

Robert Patrick grew up in the back seat of a Chevrolet in the Southwest as his parents prowled the Depression wasteland for work. Lacking the slightest socialization, he made up stories to explain the world he wandered through. Edith Hamilton's *Mythology* and the "Oz" books were the literary molds through which he funneled the forms and fantasies stimulated by radio, movies, and an unusually early puberty. Stumbling into the Caffe Cino immediately after arriving in New York in search of men, he did everything in theatre before he wrote plays. He became New York's most-produced playwright and was propelled by sheer prolificity into an international career which he jettisoned to ally himself as a lecturer with the International Thespian Society, a high-school theatre organization. After ten years visiting hundreds of secondary-school dramatic events, he decided he was being used as a token liberal to assuage the guilt of fascist tools and returned to active production. He ran the Fifth Estate Theatre in L.A., helped found La Mama Hollywood, wrote poems and essays for numerous publications. He has just completed a novel about the early days of Off-Off Broadway, *Temple Slave*. His current project is a play about Christians entitled "Where Have All the Lions Gone?" He teaches playwrighting at Elaine Gold's Corner Loft Theatre, and can usually be found at Phebe's Bar and Grill. Those interested in producing his plays may contact him c/o La Mama, 74 A E. 4th St., NYC 10003.